The Masked Riders

Bradford Scott

SAGEBRUSH
Large Print Westerns

First published in the United States by Pyramid Books

First Isis Edition
published 2020
by arrangement with
Golden West Literary Agency

A catalogue record for this book is available
from the British Library.

ISBN 978–1–78541–697–2 (pb)

Published by
F. A. Thorpe (Publishing)
Anstey, Leicestershire

Set by Words & Graphics Ltd.
Anstey, Leicestershire
Printed and bound in Great Britain by
T. J. International Ltd., Padstow, Cornwall

This book is printed on acid-free paper

CHAPTER
ONE

Sitting his tall black horse in the mouth of Persimmon Gap, Ranger Walt Slade, whom the peons of the Rio Grande River villages named *El Halcon* — the Hawk — gazed southward toward the distant Chisos Mountains.

The Chisos, or Phantoms! High, many-colored, and hazy, they bulked in a serrated mass on the horizon to the southwest. Blue, red, purple and yellow, they are the vanguard of the wildest badlands of the Texas Big Bend country. Sanctuary for hunted men and the base of operations for outlaws from both sides of the Border.

A wild and savage land of gorges and canyons and jagged mountain peaks, but also with sheltered valleys where grow the succulent needle and wheat grasses and the curly mesquite whose pods, filled with a nutritious pulp, will plump out even a gaunt old longhorn in no time.

The Bend nestles in the great bow of the Rio Grande, the string of which is the Southern Pacific Railroad. Across an awful gorge is Mexico, with the Carmen Mountains flaunting their smoldering and velvety maroon against the sky. And between the long gleam of the railroad and the silvery shimmer of the great river is the "rock," upon which the Spanish invasion broke, flowing northward on the east and west but leaving the Bend untouched so far as its civilizing effect was concerned.

It is a land where ranching never has been and doubtless never will be disturbed by the plow. A land of outlandish tradition where men bulk big, their deeds even bigger. A land to fire the imagination. Where fact and fiction merge, with little to tell the one from the other. Where anything can happen, and usually does.

All this passed through Slade's mind as he gazed down the trail that led past the Chisos, past Pommel Peak, Lost Man Peak and Mount Emory and into the solemn grandeur of an untamed wilderness where man had made but a scrape and a scratch. These were the last reaches of a very long trail Ranger Walt Slade had been riding; the trail of a hunted man; a trail marked by blood and bones and nefarious deeds.

"And if what we've learned is correct, he's been down here long enough to get well established and, no doubt, in operation," Slade remarked to Shadow, the black horse.

Shadow snorted cheerful agreement and reached for a nearby mesquite pod, which he chewed meditatively. Slade hooked one long leg over the pommel, rolled a cigarette with the slim fingers of his left hand and lounged gracefully in his double-rigged Texas saddle, strikingly in harmony with his rugged surroundings.

Very tall, more than six feet, his shoulders were broad, his chest deep, his waist lean and slender. His deeply bronzed face with its high-bridged nose, powerful chin and jaw and rather wide mouth was

2

dominated by black-lashed eyes of pale-gray — cold and reckless eyes, that nevertheless seemed to have little devils of laughter dancing in their clear depths. The kind of eyes that look out on the world with understanding and compassion and find more of good in it than evil.

Slade wore the careless but efficient garb of the rangeland: bibless overalls of blue denim — Levis they were called from the name of the first manufacturer, old Levi Straus of San Francisco — which were tucked into high-heeled half-boots of softly tanned leather, and surmounted by a well-worn blue flannel shirt with a vivid handkerchief looped about his sinewy throat. A battered, pushed-back "J.B." revealed thick, crisp black hair.

All in all, Slade looked to be a chuckline riding cowhand urged on by a roving spirit and a constant desire to see what was over the next hilltop.

Which was exactly what he wished to appear.

Glancing over his shoulder at the rising sun, he spoke to Shadow and the big black ambled down the trail.

All morning Slade rode steadily at a good pace, but did not push his mount. He forded Tornillo Creek and continued on his way. About five miles farther on he came to a fork. The main trail, he knew, led to the Grand Canyon of Santa Helena, but he turned left into a more rugged and less traveled track that he believed would eventually lead to Boquillas.

The mountain masses piled ever higher. Now the Carmens were clearly visible, their stupendous blood-colored battlements kissing the clouds. To the right frowned the Chisos, with Chillcoatl Mountain in the foreground.

Suddenly Slade lifted his head in an attitude of listening. From somewhere ahead, thin and faint with distance, like the pop and crackle of burning thorns, came a stutter of gunfire.

"Now what the devil?" he wondered aloud to Shadow. "Sounds like there might be a corpse and cartridge session going on down there. Of course it could be just a bunch of skylarking cowhands peppering holes in the clouds, but it shut off rather abruptly for that. June along, horse, and let's see what's what."

Shadow lengthened his stride. Slade gazed steadily ahead. Gunfire in this wild land usually meant trouble of some sort.

Rising straight into the crystal air, undisturbed by wind, appeared a dark column that slowly thickened and widened. Slade's eyes narrowed as he gazed at it. Down there something was burning, something big. No campfire could send up that much smoke. His voice rang out, "Trail, Shadow, trail!"

Instantly the great black extended himself. His hoofs beat a drumroll on the hard surface of the trail, his steely legs shooting back and forth like steam-driven pistons. Nostrils flaring, eyes rolling, his glorious black mane tossing and rippling in the wind of his passing, he poured his long body over the ground. Slade swayed easily in the saddle, his eyes fixed on that ominous rising column which was now less than a mile distant.

4

Shadow sped on. Here the track flowed between tall cliffs which walled it on either side. A long and gradual curve and the cliffs on the left fell back and the trail skirted a wide valley that slashed far into the hills. Not far from the valley mouth a big ranchhouse was burning fiercely, the whole first story spouting flame and smoke.

Staggering about the ranchhouse yard were two men. One was an old Mexican who hopped and limped and screamed in two languages. The other was a young cowhand, one side of whose face was crimson with blood and shredded flesh, who swore luridly.

Pulling Shadow to a slithering halt, Slade dismounted with the big black still charging at scarcely unabated speed.

"What's happened here?" he snapped.

"The Old Man — he's in there!" the cowboy gulped, gesturing wildly to the second story of the burning building. "Maybe he's dead. If he ain't, the fire'll get him."

"He come to the head of the stairs, the tall man he shoot, he fall back!" squalled the Mexican. "Me they shoot the leg as I go through the window and run. *Maledicto!*"

"He's a goner," added the cowhand.

"Maybe," Slade replied. "Anyhow, we'll try and get him out. Got a ladder?" The cowboy shook his head.

Slade strode forward a pace and took in the situation in one all-embracing glance. Directly opposite was an open second-story window. By the glare of the flames, through the swirls of smoke, he could make out the railing of the stairhead and the stout newel post to which it was attached. He studied the post a moment.

"Might work," he muttered and strode back to Shadow. Unlooping his sixty-foot sisal rope he glanced about in search of a tree or post to which he could secure the loose end of the twine. There was none in evidence.

"Guess it's up to you, feller," he told the horse and tied hard and fast to the saddle horn. Unwinding the rope, he walked toward the window until he was as close as the blistering heat would permit. Once again he studied the dimly seen newel post for an instant, measuring the distance with his eyes, and the width of the window.

It was a long throw and a difficult one, but not impossible for the man who could "dab" his tight loop onto the neck of a grazing horse without causing the others to raise their heads. A clever, underhanded cast and the loop snaked through the window and settled over the newel post. He gave it a tentative tug or two, turned to Shadow.

"Okay, feller, tighten the twine," he ordered.

Shadow moved ahead steadily until the taut rope hummed like a harp string. The whole operation hadn't taken thirty seconds. Slade sped forward, reached up and gripped the vibrating cord.

"Feller, you can't do it!" yelled the wounded cowboy. "You'll fall. You'll get burned up!"

"Remains to be seen," Slade replied and went up the slanting rope hand over hand.

As he neared the wall of the burning building, the heat struck him like the breath from a blast furnace. Almost below the window which was his goal was a first-story window through which smoke poured and flames flickered. He gasped as the flames licked upward to sear his dangling legs. The window, a good twenty feet above the ground, still looked far off.

And this was the easy half of the chore!

Panting with the heat, choking from the smoke, he made it, floundering through the opening into an inferno of smoke and heat. The smoke boiled up the stair well. Tongues of flame were lapping the landing. Blinded, he stumbled forward a step, tripped over something and nearly fell into the miniature hell that was the stairway. Reaching down, he groped the object. It was the big and bulky body of a man. A swift examination told him the heart was beating.

Holding onto his senses by sheer will power, he seized the man's arms, stretched them above his head and bound the wrists together with the tie-rope. Then, after a terrific struggle, he got the bound arms over his own head and straightened up, the flaccid form dangling down his back. Reeling and lurching, he made for the window, reached it.

Belatedly he realized that the vertical width was too narrow to let him through with the unconscious man on his back. He seized the lower sash, put forth the all of his great strength and tore it from the frame. The upper sash followed, and now the opening was large enough. With the flames darting around his legs and the floor groaning and creaking and ready to collapse,

7

he floundered through the window, a monumental task even with the rope to help him.

Finally he made it, and swung down. The rope slacked and he banged against the wall. He could hear Shadow snorting and blowing as he fought the added weight, and the scrape of his hoofs.

"Hold it, feller!" he called, his voice a hoarse croak. But Shadow heard. The rope tightened and the Ranger and his burden swung away from the burning wall. Red flashes stormed before his eyes as the jerk of the bound wrists against his throat all but throttled him. He choked, coughed, felt his senses leaving. Got to get away from the wall! Flame was pouring out the lower window. His overalls were smoldering, the heat drove through the leather of his boots.

With a mighty effort of the will, he managed to jerk one hand ahead, hold on, and jerk the other. Now he was out of the inferno of flame rolling up the wall, but the fire was licking the rope and it was still too far to drop, burdened as he was, and he was suffocating. There was a roaring in his ears, an intolerable ache in his chest. Through a fog of near exhaustion he could hear voices shouting, as if from a great distance. Dully, he wondered where they were and what they were saying. Didn't matter. One hand over the other! Hold on! One hand over the other, faltering, clutching.

Abruptly he realized that he was falling; the rope had burned through. He stiffened for the crashing impact. Instantly it came, but hardly more than a jolt. As in a dream, he realized that hands were gripping him, supporting him. Another moment and the intolerable pressure of the bound wrists against his throat ceased. He gulped a great draught of life-giving air. His vision cleared a little and he saw Shadow craning his neck toward him.

"I'm all right," he mumbled answer to anxious questions. With returning strength he lurched forward and leaned against the black's shoulder, reached out and stroked the glossy neck.

"Good horse!" he said thickly. "You did it, feller, you did it!"

The wounded cowboy was yammering excitedly. "He ain't dead! The slug just creased him! He's coming out of it!"

Feeling something like his normal self, Slade turned his attention to the rescued man. He was of middle-age, stockily built, with craggy features. The corners of his mouth had a humorous twist. His eyelids were fluttering and he was mumbling with returning consciousness. Slade examined the scalp wound just above his right temple, probed the skull with gentle, sensitive fingers.

"Nothing bad, so far as I can see," was his verdict. "Should be sitting up cussing in a few more minutes. Let him come out of it gradually. Better that way; liable to have less of a headache."

The cowhand was regarding the Ranger with a look of awe in his eyes. "Feller," he said, "I wouldn't have believed there was a man on the good Lord's green earth who could have done it. If you ever want me to do something, no matter what, just say the word."

"Thanks," Slade smiled. "Now let's have a look at your face."

From his saddle pouches he took a roll of bandage, a clean handkerchief, adhesive tape and a jar of antiseptic ointment. He wiped away the blood to expose a jagged tear extending from almost the corner of the mouth to the angle of the jaw.

"I'm afraid it'll leave a bad scar, but otherwise nothing much to it," he said. "I'll do the best I can with it. If you manage to see a doctor before too long and have him stitch it, the scar won't be so prominent."

"There's one at Boquillas, which ain't so far off," said the puncher. "I'll try and see him tomorrow."

"Do that," Slade advised. He smeared the wound with ointment, deftly taped a pad into place.

"A slug fired at close range is pretty hot and usually cauterizes the wound fairly well," he observed. "Should be no bad after-effects."

He turned to the old Mexican. "And now, *hombre*, we'll give your leg a once-over," he said.

The old fellow pulled up his overall leg to reveal a flesh wound in the calf. Ointment, a pad and a few strips of tape quickly took care of that. Just as he was finishing the chore, Slade heard a rousing burst of profanity behind him. He turned to see the man he had rescued from the burning ranchhouse, now but a mass of flame and smoke, sitting up, looking dazed and swearing with amazing fluency.

"Take it easy, sir," he counseled. "You'll start your head bleeding again."

The owner of the head in question glared at him and opened his mouth to make further pungent remarks, but the young puncher poured forth a torrent of speech. The oldster listened open-mouthed and when the other paused for breath he turned to Slade.

"Son," he said heavily, "reckon about all I can do is say much obliged, but I won't forget it, I won't forget it. My name's Randal, George Randal, and if you'll help me onto my pins, I sorta hanker to shake hands."

Slade did so, lifting him lightly to his feet, supplied his name, and Randal stuck out a huge paw and shook hands with a firm grip. Looking him over closely, *El Halcon* decided it wouldn't be hard to like George Randal.

Randal glanced at the others. "So you fellers got it, too, eh?" he observed. "Why didn't the blankety-blanks kill you?"

"Me, I go through the window and hide in the grass," said the Mexican.

"And I reckon they figured I was done for when I pitched over on my head, bleeding like a stuck pig," the cowboy chimed in. "I came out of it in time to hear them hightailing and see the ranchhouse burning like crazy. I didn't know what to do. I knew you were upstairs but couldn't figure how to get to you. Then this big feller came a-larrupin' up, and I told you how he hauled you out. Slade, ain't it you said? I'd sorta like to shake hands, too. My handle's Yost. Harvey Yost."

"And I am Felipe, I cook," said the Mexican, shaking hands in turn.

"And now," Slade suggested, "suppose you tell me what this is all about."

CHAPTER
TWO

"It was this way," explained Randal. "I sold a small bunch of cows to a buyer in Boquillas — beef for the Terlingua mines — and headed home with the dinero of two thousand pesos. Harve and Felipe came along. The rest of my boys stayed over in Boquillas for a mite of celebration. I stowed the money in the safe in the living room and went upstairs to rest a mite. Figured to pack it up to Marathon and the bank in the next few days. The blankety-blank Faceless Riders must have caught on I was packing it from Boquillas. Anyhow, they jumped the ranchhouse. I heard the shooting and ran out of my room to the stairs. Got a glimpse of the hellions and then the world blew up around my ears. That's all I remember till I come to out here."

"I see," Slade nodded. "And who are the Faceless Riders?"

"A blankety-blank owlhoot bunch that's been sashayin' all over this section for the past six months, robbing and killing," stormed Randal. "Nobody has ever got a look at their faces. They always have white rags tied tight over them, with eye-holes. That's how they got that monicker; some loco horntoad hung it onto 'em. It does sort of fit, though. The way they wear those rags makes it look like they really haven't any faces, especially at night."

"I wonder why they fired the ranchhouse?" Slade remarked.

"Just plain cussedness," Randal replied. "They do things like that out of pure senseless deviltry. The big tall hellion who 'pears to run the bunch seems to get a real wallop outa making people suffer. Over in Mexico, across from Boquillas, Texas, they pegged a poor jigger over an anthill for no reason at all, so far as anybody knows. If some *vaqueros* hadn't happened by just in time, he'd have been plumb eat up alive. Very nearly killed him as it was. They stripped two other fellers naked and hung 'em up by the thumbs in the hot sun. They both died. Another feller they shot half a dozen times through his breast, hung him up and put flowers in the bullet holes. Oh, they're a bunch of sidewinders for fair!"

Slade nodded, his face thoughtful, his eyes pale and cold. It was a long time before George Randal forgot the look in those eyes.

"Gave me the creeps," he confided to his range boss, later. "Looked like knife points in the sun. A plumb fine feller, but I'd sooner rile a den full of grizzlies than him."

Randal gazed a moment at the ruins of the ranchhouse, which was burning down to a smolder.

"Well, the casa's a goner," he observed. "Have to build another one soon as we can get stuff from Boquillas and Marathon. Lucky, the storeroom back of the barn is full of chuck and we can throw together a surrounding and eat in the bunkhouse. Plenty of fire to cook it over, anyhow," he added, with a dreary laugh. "But I reckon we're lucky to be alive, and they couldn't pack off the spread. The old Walking R is still here, and she's a good one, just about the best in the Big Bend, so I won't complain too much. You'll spend the night with us, of course, and a lot longer, I hope. Plenty of room in the bunkhouse tonight. We'll make out. Stir your stumps, Felipe, if you can still walk, and fix up something to eat. I'm gaunt as a gutted sparrow."

"I walk," said Felipe, and suited the action to the word, albeit with a considerable limp.

While Randal supervised the preparation of the meal, Slade gave Shadow a good rubdown before stabling him.

"Horse," he said, "we're on the right track. There's no doubt but that big tall hellion they talk about is Veck Sosna, the Panhandle outlaw leader of the Comancheros who raised so much heck in the Canadian Valley and gave us the slip when we thought we had him corralled. Nobody else would pull the outlandish stunts these Faceless Riders, as they call them, are going in for. Yes, it's Sosna, the sidewinder we're trailing. Been a long trail. From the Panhandle to east Texas, down to the Gulf and now over here in southwest Texas. He can't go much farther, unless he slides across into Mexico and hightails south. He'll slide over now and then, all right, but I figure he won't stay and he won't head south. Not unless we're right on his tail and he's making a run for it. Anyhow, where he goes we go, official authority or not. He's our meat, horse, and we're going to drop the loop on him, sooner or later."

El Halcon versus Veck Sosna! A saga of the West that would be talked about for many a year! The most famous of the Texas Rangers and the deadliest, smartest and cruellest of Texas outlaws!

Despite the handicap of their wounds, Yost and Felipe managed to throw together an appetizing supper of which all partook with relish. Randal and the others made light of their injuries and Slade knew there was little danger of these rugged outdoor men suffering any ill after-effects. You can't be sure you've killed a Texan until you have him buried, and even then he's liable to climb up the handle of the shovel and belt you one.

Later, Slade discovered what he considered to be evidence to bolster his belief that the leader of the Faceless Riders was none other than Veck Sosna, the man he had trailed all over Texas. The ranchhouse had burned down to smoldering ruins, mostly ashes with here and there a beam or king post still flickering. The big old iron safe Randal said the outlaws looted was standing lopsidedly in the shallow basement, the door wide open. Slade studied it by the last rays of the setting sun, getting as close as he could against the heat.

"Was that safe locked?" he asked of Randal, who had joined him.

"Yep, she was locked," the rancher replied. "Why?"

"Interesting," Slade answered musingly. "It shows no sign of being forced. The lock is undamaged, and so is the door. Looks like the combination was worked.

Unusual procedure for an owlhoot bunch in this section. Dynamite or a sledge hammer is more their style."

After his initial brush with Veck Sosna in the Panhandle, Slade had found out all he could about the elusive outlaw leader and his past. He knew that Sosna was an educated man and had studied medicine, but he was somewhat surprised to learn that he was a university graduate, *summa cum laude*. Very likely there was hardly anything Veck Sosna didn't know something about; not unreasonable that safe cracking might be one of his accomplishments.

"That bunch aren't ordinary bush poppers," Randal declared with conviction. "The feller at the head of 'em has brains."

Slade nodded soberly. With that he was wholly in accord, if his suspicions were well grounded and the leader of the Faceless Riders really was Veck Sosna.

As they sat on the bunkhouse steps, smoking, Randal told Slade what he knew about the depredations of the Faceless Riders.

"Grabbed a mine payroll at Terlingua — better'n two thousand pesos," said the rancher. "Killed the paymaster and a clerk. Robbed a bank at Presidio, over to the west, shot the cashier between the eyes. Darned if they didn't cross the Rio Grande the next day and rob one in Ojinaga, the Mexican town across from Presidio. Killed a man there. Slid up to Marathon and stuck up a saloon. Took the payday take and a couple of cases of whiskey. Shot the owner twice, but he didn't die. The spreads to the east of here have been losing

17

cows, plenty. Oh, they swallerfork all over the map. Hasn't been anything like it in this section since the days of Bajo El Sol and his Comanche raiders, and they mostly hit Mexico."

"Any notion how many in the bunch?" Slade asked.

"'Pears to be a dozen or so, but there might be more," Randal answered. "Hard to tell if it's always the same hellions, with their faces wrapped up like they are. The big tall sidewinder who seems to run things is always along, though."

He would be! was Slade's unspoken thought.

"Oh yes, and they wrecked the Sunrise Limited, too," added Randal. "Planted dynamite and blew up the track in front of the train. Busted open the express car door with a stick of dynamite and blew the express messenger to bits. Come to think of it, I believe I heard they worked the combination of the express car safe or drilled it; didn't blow it or hammer it open. Uh-huh, I'm pretty sure I heard that."

Slade nodded. The account closely paralleled the methods used by Sosna and his Comancheros in the course of a train robbery in the Panhandle. Yes, it was tieing up; the leader of the Faceless Riders was the man he sought. Caught up with the sidewinder at last. All he had to do was drop a loop on him. Which, judging from past performance, was, he wryly admitted, liable to be considerable of a chore. Oh, well, the hellion's luck couldn't hold out for ever.

Or was it luck? Walt Slade didn't believe it was. Rather, it was brains and ability, reckless courage and a hair-trigger mind that assessed and evaluated a situation with speed and accuracy and took instant advantage of all possible breaks. *That* was Veck Sosna!

Everybody went to bed early, for it had been quite a day for all concerned. Despite the fact that his legs were sore from the scorching they received, his hands likewise from the effects of the rope, Slade slept soundly in a comfortable bunk, getting the first good night's rest he'd had in days. Morning found him fit for anything.

Harve Yost's face was so sore when he got up that eating was difficult and laughter out of the question, while Felipe was limping badly and vividly expressing his opinion of things in general in two languages with a few pungent Yaqui expletives dropped in for good measure. After some activity and a good breakfast, however, both perked up quite a bit. Randal appeared to suffer no ill effects from the slug that nicked his scalp and knocked him unconscious.

Shortly after noon, the rest of the Walking R hands rode in from Boquillas shouting questions and volleying profanity. They were mostly young punchers, but there were a couple of old gray-heads, somewhat the worse for wear but still quite chipper.

After being regaled with a vivid account of what happened, all solemnly shook hands with Slade.

"We'd sure hated to lose him," one said. "No man ever worked for a better boss. Stick with us, Slade. We can use you, and you won't be sorry."

One of the riders was a young Mexican *vaquero* who stared at Slade open-mouthed. Slade, his cold eyes all kindness, voiced a Spanish greeting, which caused the *vaquero* to smile happily. A little later Slade himself suppressed a smile as he noticed him talking excitedly in low tones with Randal. He was not surprised when the ranch owner drew him aside.

"Son," Randal said, "are you *El Halcon?*"

"Been called that," Slade admitted.

"I've heard quite a bit about *El Halcon*," Randal said, "and just a little while ago I heard a lot more. According to Pedro Gonzales over there" — he gestured to the young Mexican — "you must just about be the best. And after what you did yesterday, I'm inclined to agree with Pedro."

"Thank you, sir," Slade replied. "I fear Pedro sort of exaggerates."

"Not for my money he don't," Randal declared sturdily. "I'll string right along with him. And I sure hope you'll decide to sign on with me."

"Even though I am *El Halcon?*" Slade asked with a smile.

"As I said, I've heard a mite about *El Halcon*," Randal replied. "I've heard he has quite a few killings to his credit, and I reckon credit is just about the right word. For so far as I've been able to learn, all the hellions he cashed in had a killing long overdue. Anyhow, you're the bully boy with the glass eye for my money, as the saying goes, and nothing would please me more than to have you sign up with me."

"I may," Slade said, and meant it. "But first I'd like to ride to Boquillas for a day or two."

20

"Fine!" said Randal. "We'll ride together in the morning, if you can hold up for that long. I'll have to contract for materials for a new ranchhouse. Should be able to get most of what I need in Boquillas, Mexico, across the river, though I may have to go to Marathon for some things. Okay?"

"In the morning, we'll make it," Slade agreed. "I'm in no great rush."

"Fine!" Randal repeated, adding in low tones and with a chuckle, "I sorta feel the need of a bodyguard tomorrow. You see, those hellions didn't get the whole two thousand. One thousand was in gold ten-dollar pieces and I put that in the safe. My cash-in-hand was just about cleaned out. You know everybody in this section likes to be paid in 'hard money,' not paper. It was in a sack with the bank's markings and sealed. Reckon when they grabbed that they figured they got it all, but they didn't. I had the other thousand in my wallet in big bills and was packing that on me. That's what I figured to take to the bank. Got it right here." He produced a fat wallet, still chuckling.

"But don't you figure you may be taking a chance, confiding in *El Halcon*?" Slade asked seriously but with his eyes twinkling.

Randal thrust the wallet at him. "Here, take it and put it in your pocket," he said. "I've a notion it will be safer with you packing it."

Slade laughingly shook his head. "I've a notion it'll fit better in your pocket," he declined. However, he was quickly serious again. "Mr. Randal, if the bunch was able to learn you were packing the money to the

21

ranchhouse, isn't it logical to believe that they also learned the amount?"

"Why, I reckon so," Randal replied. "Why?"

"Because," Slade said, "it's quite likely that they were considerably riled when they counted it and learned they'd gotten only half of what you were packing. And, judging from their reputation and their way of doing things, it is not unreasonable to believe that they might try to even up the score after they learn you weren't cashed in. They appear able to learn things mighty fast."

"By gosh!" exclaimed Randal. "I never thought of that. It would be just like the hellions. Darned if I don't believe you're right."

"I rather think I am," Slade said. "We'll just keep it in mind."

Before going to sleep, Slade carefully reviewed recent happenings. He was amused and pleased at Randal's reaction to learning he was the "notorious" *El Halcon*.

Due to his habit of working undercover whenever possible and often not revealing his true status as a law enforcement officer, Walt Slade had built up a peculiar dual reputation. By those who knew the truth he was looked upon as the smartest and ablest, as well as the most fearless of the famed Texas Rangers. Others, including some puzzled sheriffs and other peace officers, maintained profanely that he was just a blasted owlhoot too smart to get caught, so far.

Slade did nothing to disillusion them, although he knew that his reputation as an outlaw laid him open to grave personal danger.

"Sometime, some trigger-happy deputy marshal will cut down on you without warning," Captain Jim McNelty, the famous commander of the Border Battalion, was wont to declare. "Or some gunslinger out to get a reputation will plug you in the back and then swear he outdrew *El Halcon*."

"Hasn't happened so far," Slade would reply cheerfully. "And it opens up avenues of information that would be closed to a known Ranger. Besides, owlhoots will sometimes take a chance and tip their hand, thinking they just have to deal with one of their own ilk."

Captain Jim would grumble, but not specifically order Slade to change his tactics. So as *El Halcon* he went his merry way, satisfied with the present and giving scant thought to the future.

CHAPTER
THREE

Early the following morning, Slade and Randal set out for Boquillas under a sky of brilliant blue washed with golden sunshine.

"She ain't much of a town, Boquillas, Texas," observed Randal, "but Boquillas, Mexico, across the river, is a whizzer. A booming mining community. That's where the boys usually go for their celebrating, although things can be a mite lively on this side of the river at times. Closer than Marathon, up to the north, where there's always some sort of a humdinger cutting loose. Well, we turn left here. Then right, then left again, then a couple of miles or so to Boquillas. Isn't over far, but rough going."

It was, Slade was willing to concede. On every hand towered mountain crags, raking the sky with stony fingers. The trail ran between tall cliffs or heavy stands of thorn brush, with here and there open spaces strewn with boulders and talus fallen from the cliffs. No sound broke the stillness save the twitterings of birds and the gentle soughing of the wind through the branches.

Randal chatted animatedly of this and that, but Slade was mostly silent, his eyes continually studying the terrain ahead. This was owlhoot land, the only law that which they carried in their holsters. No movement of bird on the wing or little creature in the brush escaped his notice, and all such movements were carefully analyzed and their reason sought for. The strange and unexplainable sixth sense that births in men who ride much alone with danger as a constant stirrup companion, which warns of peril when none, apparently, exists, was highly developed in *El Halcon*. And now that voiceless monitor was setting up an unheard but very real clamor. Slade felt his nerves tensing, and every sense was at razor-edge alertness. With nothing tangible on which to base it, the feeling that something untoward was in the making grew and persisted.

From time to time they would top a rise from the crest of which they could see for some distance in every direction. But Slade also knew that they could be *seen* for some distance from every direction. After each, his vigilance increased.

They rounded a sweeping bend, beyond which the trail ran straight for nearly a mile. As they reached the apex of the curve and could see down the straightaway, a coyote burst from a thicket several hundred yards ahead, streaked across the trail, looking over its shoulder, and vanished into the brush on the far side. Slade shot out a long arm, gripped Randal's bridle iron and jerked his mount to a standstill. Shadow, in obedience to knee pressure, instantly halted.

"What the —" began the startled rancher.

"Over to the side, against the brush," Slade snapped.

Randal obeyed, looking bewildered, hugging the thorny growth.

"What is it?" he asked. "What's the matter?"

Slade replied obliquely. "Wonder what started old fuzz-tail off like that?"

"Maybe a mountain lion," Randal guessed. Slade shook his head.

"He'd play tag through the brush with a lion, knowing that with his speed he'd have nothing to fear, even if the lion was trying to tackle him, which would be highly unlikely. Lions don't go for coyote meat unless they're starving, and there's no reason for them to be starving in this sort of country. He was sleeping in that thicket and something he's very much afraid of scared him bad and set him high-tailing."

"But if not a lion, what?" asked Randal. "He'd hardly run from a snake or another wolf."

"I don't know for sure," Slade answered, "but I do know that riding down that straight stretch we'd be setting quail for anybody holed up in the brush."

Randal looked decidedly startled. "You mean somebody might be there waiting to plug us?" he demanded. "Maybe some of those blasted Faceless Riders?"

"I don't know for sure," Slade repeated, "but you'll recall I said that when they learned they'd only gotten half of the two thousand they might be out to even the score. If they learned you were alive, and they seem to be able to learn anything they desire to, it's not unreasonable to think that they'd figure you'd be heading for Boquillas soon to purchase materials for a new ranchhouse, and would be packing the thousand along. They *might* make another try for it."

Darned if that doesn't seem to make sense," sputtered Randal. "What the devil we going to do?"

Slade was still studying the trail ahead. "I think," he said, "that, if you don't mind taking a chance, it would be a good idea to leave the horses here in the brush and then slide down through the growth on foot. If there is anybody in that thicket, we may be able to get in behind them — they'll be watching the trail — and give them a surprise."

"I'm for it," Randal declared heartily. "Nothing would suit me better than a chance to line sights with those blankety-blanks."

Slade studied a tall peak to the west for a moment, in relation to its direction from the thicket from which the coyote had appeared. His gaze went back to the trail, estimated the distance.

"Okay," he said. "I think I've got that brush heap pretty well lined up. Let's go."

He turned the big black into the tangle of growth. Shadow didn't like it but with a disgusted snort obeyed orders. Randal's mount hung back, but a mite of tickling with the spurs decided him it was best to go ahead. Slade dropped the split reins to the ground. Randal tied his cayuse securely to a low branch.

"I don't think they could have seen us from down there, if somebody is on the watch," Slade said. "But we're taking no chances. Go slow and easy, and for Pete's sake don't make a noise, or we may get a surprise *we* won't like."

"I'm pretty good at brush work — did a lot of hunting in my day," Randal replied.

With the greatest caution they stole forward, careful to kick no stone, to tread on no dry and fallen branch, gently moving obstructing twigs aside. From time to time, through rifts in the growth, Slade could see the peak to the west. It was in line with the thicket where the coyote appeared and was the apex of the triangle he had plotted in his mind, of which he and Randal were the foot of the moving leg. As they progressed, the angle between the two imaginary lines steadily narrowed. When it ceased altogether and the line merged, they should be directly opposite the point in the brush which was their goal.

"Getting close," Slade breathed. "Stop a minute and listen."

Standing motionless, they strained their ears. Suddenly Slade heard a sound, a soft thump followed by a faint, musical jingle.

"A horse stamped its foot and shook its bridle irons," he whispered to his companion. "Somebody in there, all right. Another dozen paces or so and we should be in line with them. Slow and easy, now."

They resumed their snail-creep, pausing after every few steps to peer and listen. It was ticklish and nerve-straining business. For all they knew they had been spotted on the curve, the cunning outlaws had divined what they would do and were ready and waiting for them. The first warning that this was so might well be a blast of gunfire.

Step by slow step! Slade got a final glimpse of the peak which was his guidepost and touched his companion's arm. Randal instantly halted. Slade pointed toward the trail, some little distance to the west. Randal nodded his understanding, and they turned in that direction. Again they heard the jingle of bridle irons, very close now; but the growth was thick and tall and they could see nothing.

Again the slow crawl, with nerves strained to the breaking point. Slade banked his hopes on the outlaws' being intent on the trail and giving no heed to what went on in the growth behind them. If he was right, okay. If he was wrong . . .

The growth began to thin. A final breathless advance and he saw, in a little cleared space, three men standing motionless and peering through a screen of leaves up the trail. Two held rifles at the ready. The third, somewhat behind the others, had nothing in his hands, but he wore double holsters.

Slade hesitated. The devils were bent on snake-blooded murder, nothing less. But he was a law enforcement officer. His duty was to give them a chance to surrender, even with the odds against him. And then the unpredictable happened.

Randal had drawn his old Smith & Wesson .44. He made the mistake of cocking it. The sharp double click reached the ears of the nearest drygulcher. He whirled at the sound, hands streaking to his guns.

Slade drew and shot, left and right. The outlaw reeled back and fell, hands still gripping the butts of his guns. His companions whirled, rifles blazing. Lead fanned Slade's face. A slug ripped his shirt sleeve and nicked the flesh of his arm. Another grazed the top of his shoulder. Randal's old Smith cut loose with a booming roar. Back and forth spurted the lances of flame, knifing through the whirl of powder smoke. Slade lowered his guns and peered through the fog at the three figures sprawled on the ground. He began ejecting the spent shells from his Colts and spoke, his voice hard, metallic.

"Well, I guess that settles that. You all right?"

"Little hunk of meat knocked out of my hand, but nothing to worry about," Randal replied, wringing the blood-dripping member. The gaze he bent on Slade was an expression of awe.

"Son, how the devil did you do it?" he asked. "You had your irons out and going before I could pull trigger. How *did* you do it?"

"Perhaps you're a mite slow," Slade smiled reply, slipping fresh cartridges into the cylinders of his guns.

"I sorta got a reputation for *not* being slow," Randal said. "Come to think of it, I rec'lect something that's said about *El Halcon:* 'The singingest man in the whole Southwest, with the fastest gunhand!' Can't say as to the singing part, seeing as I ain't heard you warble, but I'm sure plumb in accord with the other half. Gentlemen, hush!"

Slade laughed and holstered his guns. "Let's see what we bagged," he suggested.

"Ornery looking scums," Randal growled as they turned the bodies over and peered at the dead faces.

"Yes," Slade agreed, "but judging from appearances a bit more intelligent than the average Border scum. We'll find out what they've got on them. May tell us something."

He began turning out the dead outlaws' pockets, revealing various odds and ends of no significance and a sizeable sum of money. Then he struck paydirt, drawing forth a bit of stiff white cloth neatly folded. Shaking it out revealed that it was a hood that would fit snugly over a man's head, supplied with eye-holes cut in the fabric. Randal swore sulphurously.

"The Faceless Riders, sure as shootin'!" he exclaimed. "Look, here's another of the blasted things."

"Yes, looks that way," Slade agreed soberly. "Reckon my hunch was a straight one."

Randal regarded him in silence for a moment.

"Son," he said soberly, "if you hadn't showed up in this section when you did, I'd need to be a cat to survive. Anyhow, as things stand, if I was one, I'd have only seven lives left out of the nine. If it hadn't been for you, I would have barged right into that drygulching."

"Perhaps," Slade acceded, "You haven't had as much experience at this sort of thing as *El Halcon*."

"Yes, as *El Halcon*," Randal repeated. "Well, all I can say is I hope this section grows a whole herd of *El Halcons*. We can use them."

"Remember, you've seen only one side of *El Halcon*," Slade said gravely, but with dancing eyes.

"Guess there's only one side to see, and I've seen it, all right," Randal grunted. "What shall we do with this dinero. Looks like there's several hundred dollars here."

"Put it in your pocket," Slade directed. "You'll notice it's all in gold. Chances are it's part of the thousand they took out of your safe."

"You've earned a cut," Randal declared. Slade smiled and shook his head.

"Got a few pesos salted away against a rainy day, and you don't need much money in my line of business," he declined.

Randal shook his head dubiously but pocketed the money. "And what about these carcasses?" he asked.

"We'll leave them where they are for the time being," Slade decided. "Later perhaps we'll notify the sheriff and he can dispose of them as he sees fit. Now let's locate the horses and get the rigs off them so they can fend for themselves."

They quickly discovered the outlaws' mounts, good-looking animals. Two bore meaningless Mexican brands, but the third boasted a neatly stamped LC.

"Interesting," Slade commented. "That's a Panhandle burn. Of course, though, it may mean nothing. Horses can be bought or traded or stolen and sometimes show up a long ways from their foaling ground. Well, I guess this takes care of everything here and we might as well be on our way."

"Don't reckon there are any more of the sidewinders slithering around nearby?" Randal remarked apprehensively.

"Not likely," Slade replied, "but we'll keep our eyes open. Chances are these three were detailed for the chore, and no more. Let's go."

CHAPTER
FOUR

Retrieving their horses, they resumed their journey, reaching Boquillas Pass without incident. Here the route followed an old Indian and smuggler trail. Directly above, Randal pointed out a stone barricade.

"Was built during one of the Border wars, long ago," he explained. "Been a heap of fighting in this gulch. A little bit ahead is Dead Man's Turn. Called that because a jigger was killed there during one of the rukuses. From there you can see Boquillas, Mexico, and get a good look at the Carmen Mountains. Worth looking at from there, all bloody red and smoky purple. Boquillas means 'little mouths' in Mexican talk and they call Boquillas Canyon that because it's plumb narrow, just a big crack in the rock of the mountain wall. The river bed is nearly two thousand feet above sea level, while the rim of the canyon is nearly four thousand. Quite a drop to the water — coupla thousand feet. A feller would get hungry before he landed."

The trail ran directly into Boquillas, Texas, which proved to be a scattered hamlet of 'dobes and old houses. Across the wide flood of the Rio Grande was the busy and bustling mining town of Boquillas, Mexico.

"Over there is where we're headed for," Randal said. "I want to have a little gab with my old *amigo*, Ramos Alvarez, the manager of the big Puerto Rico silver mine. He can dig up most of the stuff I need and have it sent to the spread. Easy to cross. The creek is low."

The Rio Grande was low, and some distance out from the bank was profane proof of the fact. A huge flat-bottom boat loaded with silver ore was stuck in the mud, while the cursing boatmen labored futilely to get it afloat.

"They have plenty of trouble when the water is down," Randal observed. "The ore is ferried across and sent north by wagons to the stamp mills. Those old scows get stuck every so often and it is one devil of a chore to pry 'em loose from the mud. Alvarez will be fit to be hogtied about now."

Slade nodded thoughtfully. He was surveying the immediate terrain, noting that a little west of the town the river bank was high and rocky. A similar condition prevailed on the Mexican side of the stream.

Shortly before his father died, after suffering financial reverses that entailed the loss of his ranch, Walt Slade had graduated from a famous college of engineering. His plan had been to take a post graduate course to round out his education and better fit him for the profession he intended to make his life work. Under the circumstances, this became impossible for the time being. So when Captain Jim McNelty, the Commander of the Border Battalion of the Texas Rangers, suggested

34

that Slade come into the Rangers for a while and pursue his studies in spare time, young Walt, who had worked some with Captain Jim during summer vacations, thought the idea a good one. Long since he had gotten more from private study than he could have from the postgrad. But meanwhile, Ranger work had gotten a strong hold on him and he was loath to sever connections with the illustrious body of peace officers. He'd stick to the Rangers for the present; plenty of time to be an engineer later.

His engineering knowledge had frequently been of value during his work as a Ranger, and here Slade believed might be another opportunity to use that knowledge to advantage. So he studied the physical features of the vicinity with the understanding eye of an engineer.

"I think I'll have a little talk with *Senor* Alvarez," he remarked to Randal as they put their horses to the water.

The rancher shot him a curious glance but only said, "You'll find Al easy to talk to. He's a prime jigger."

They negotiated the crossing without difficulty and repaired to the mine officers.

As Randal predicted, Alvarez, a distinguished-looking and handsome middle-aged man, was in anything but a good temper. However, he greeted Randal warmly, and after the rancher had talked a little, he shook hands with Slade a second time.

"I'd have been desolated if something bad had happened to my old friend," he said. "Mr. Slade, you have made of me a friend for life."

"What's got you worked up, Al?" asked Randal. "You look as peeved as a teased snake."

"It's those confounded ore boats," growled Alvarez, who spoke colloquial English. "They keep sticking in the mud, and I'm already behind in my shipments. It's enough to drive a man out of his mind."

Slade turned to face the mine official. "*Senor* Alvarez," he asked, "did you ever hear of an overhead conveyor system?"

"Why, I think I have," replied Alvarez, "although I never saw one. Why?"

"Because," Slade said, "that is precisely what you need here. With one in operation, you would be independent of weather and water. All that's needed is a tower on the river bank here and one across the river in Texas. The towers would support a cable stretched across the river, upon which the ore buckets would travel by means of pulleys, to dump their contents directly into the wagons. A steam boiler and a winding machine would supply the necessary power. The cost would not be prohibitive and the investment would pay off big in the end."

Alvarez rolled and lighted a husk cigarette and smoked thoughtfully before replying.

"It sounds good," he conceded at length, "but how would we go about acquiring such a machine? We are backward down here, in some ways, and have a habit of doing things as our fathers did them before us. I am a mining man but I am not familiar with such mechanical contrivances."

"There is a firm in Laredo, Texas, that would supply all that's necessary," Slade replied. "They would accept the order by telegraph."

"I see," nodded Alvarez. Again he was silent, puffing on his cigarette. Tossing away the butt, he asked another question.

"Could you give me an estimate of the cost?"

Taking pencil and paper, Slade did some figuring. Finally he passed the totals to the manager. Alvarez studied them.

"We can swing that, all right," he said. Abruptly he raised his eyes to Slade's.

"And if I decide to go through with the project, Mr. Slade, will you consent to attend to the installing?" he asked.

Slade reflected quickly. It would provide him with an opportunity and an excuse for being in Boquillas. And he believed the twin towns would be an excellent vantage point from which to possibly get a line on Veck Sosna and his raiders. Very likely they frequented Boquillas, Mexico. At least it was the sort of a pueblo where information could be picked up.

"The Laredo people will send along a corps of trained mechanics to do the chore of installing the system," he replied. "But I will agree to supervise the installation and make sure it is in perfect working order, if you desire me to."

"Fine!" said Alvarez. "And will you also attend to procuring the necessary materials? You will know what to order. I don't." Slade nodded.

"Fine!" Alvarez repeated. "I will give you authority to order everything needed, in my name." He grinned. "If George recommends you, I guess you're trustworthy enough."

"Well, I already owe him a couple of lives, and I'm plumb ready to trust him with what's left," Randal put in.

"That's enough for me," Alvarez chuckled. "You're on the payroll, Mr. Slade, as of today."

"And there goes my chance of hiring the best tophand in Texas!" lamented Randal.

"The chore won't take overly long," Slade reassured him. "Very well, *Senor* Alvarez. I will ride to Marathon without delay and put in the order."

"Take your time," said Alvarez. "We've done things by hand here for a good many years, so a day or two won't matter much one way or the other. We'll fix up the little matter of your salary and then suppose we seal the bargain with a drink and a bite to eat at one of the *cantinas? A fiesta* in town tonight and things are liable to be lively. Not that it's dull at any time. If the local *muchachos* can't raise enough of a rukus, cowboys from across the river are always ready to lend a hand."

"Something in the nature of an understatement," Randal commented. Alvarez chuckled.

"Got a few papers to file and the safe to lock, then I'll be right with you," he said. Slade and Randal sauntered out into the blue dusk and stood gazing at the mighty wall of the Chisos outlined against the blossoming stars in the east.

"Son," the rancher said, "you've sure got a way with you. Anybody who can talk an old stock Spanish-Mexican into doing something new has to have."

"Mexicans are changing," Slade replied. "They're becoming more progressive by the day. Time will come when down here will be a great progressive nation which will stand shoulder to shoulder with America in a day of need."

"I've a notion you're right," conceded Randal. "Hello, A1, all set to go?"

The Mexican town was gay and colorful. A big market housed venders of meats, vegetables, fruits, and exotic foods. Also jewelry, perfumes, pottery and basketware. There were also garish copies of Aztec art, woven garments of vivid hues, *serapes*, or blankets, and steeple-crowned *sombreros* encrusted with silver. Randal chuckled.

"The cowhands buy that stuff for their girls," he remarked. "Some of it is right purty, don't you think?"

Dressed in *charro* costumes that included gay *sombreros*, embroidered *serapes* and velvet pantaloons, wandering troubadours strummed guitars and sang the folk songs of Mexico. Pausing at street corners, they were soon the center of eager throngs, applauding vigorously.

"This one can sing!" Alvarez suddenly exclaimed. "Plays well, too. Let's stop and listen to him."

They pushed their way to the front, until they were close to the singer, a handsome young Mexican with much Indian blood, whose black eyes snapped and sparkled. Suddenly his gaze fixed on Slade's face. He ceased in the middle of his song, dropped the guitar to his side and bowed low, his sombrero sweeping the dust.

"*Capitan!*" he exclaimed. "*Ai!* I knew not you were here, else I would not have raised my voice in your presence. *Capitan*, will you not sing for us, as only *El Halcon* can sing?"

A murmur ran through the crowd which was abruptly silent. Men bent forward to gaze eagerly at Slade.

"*El Halcon!* It is indeed he! *El Halcon*, the friend of the lowly, the champion of the troubled, the wronged, the oppressed! Truly this is a day of *fiesta*, now that *El Halcon* is here!"

"Heck and blazes!" Slade heard Ramos Alvarez mutter. He stifled a grin with difficulty.

The voices grew still louder as the troubadour thrust his guitar at Slade.

"Sing, *Capitan*! Sing for us! Laughing and cheering, the throng closed in on Slade and his companions. "We will not let you go, *Capitan*, until you sing!"

Randal added his voice to the others. "Come on, son, give us one," he said. "If that feller says you can, I reckon there ain't any doubt about it. Come on, let's hear what the singingest man in the whole Southwest can do."

"Yes, Mr. Slade, please do," Alvarez chimed in. "I love good music."

"Well, I guess I have no choice, if we are to get anything to eat tonight," Slade acceded. He accepted the guitar, ran his slim fingers over the strings and

40

played a soft prelude. Then he threw back his black head and sang, a song the troubadours loved, which had gushed from the dream-filled heart of some unknown poet who caught the hopes and the fears, the joys and the sorrows, the hopeless aspirations and the quiet faith of a people in a net of words and uplifted them on wings of song. And as the great thundering baritone-bass filled the night with melody, men and women stood entranced, hands clasped as in prayer.

The music ceased in a final exquisite breath of perfect harmony and Slade stood smiling at the storm of "vivas."

"Good gosh!" exclaimed Randal. "You've emptied the big *cantina* across the way. Even the bartenders are on the street!"

The cheers continued, and the troubadour's *sombrero*, which he had placed on the ground, was overflowing with coins.

Slade noted that there was a fair sprinkling of Texas cowhands in the crowd, who were shouting, "Give us another, feller, give us another!" So he gave them another; a rollicking old ballad of the range:

> Just a-ridin' and a-ropin'
> And a-brandin' all day long!
> Just a-waitin' for the campfire
> And a chance to raise a song!
>
> While the moon is standin' night-guard
> On a herd of restless stars
> Way up yonder on the Big Range

Where there aren't no corral bars!

Just a-sweatin' and a-toilin'
And a-eatin' dust and sun;
Then to town and raise Old Harry
When the round-up days are done!

Again a thunder of applause and a waving of hands. "*Gracias, amigos, gracias!*" Slade called reply and handed the guitar to its owner.

Ramos Alvarez was gazing fixedly at Slade. "*El Halcon*," he said. "I've heard a lot about *El Halcon*. Yes, quite a lot."

"And are you still satisfied to have me install your conveyor system?" Slade asked.

"No, I am not," Alvarez declared positively.

George Randal bristled. But before he could bellow a protest, Alvarez continued.

"I'll not be satisfied until you sign a ten-year contract at a good salary and stay here with me, instead of mavericking around and taking the chance of getting into serious trouble some time. Let's go eat!"

As they pushed their way through the still applauding crowd, Randal observed, "Al, I believe that in your old age you're actually getting out of the terrapin-brain class."

CHAPTER
FIVE

The *cantina*, quite a large room, tastefully decorated, was softly lighted but not gloomy. The proprietor, rotund and jovial, came hurrying to greet them.

"The business I lose," he said, "but gladly would I lose even the *cantina* to hear *El Halcon* sing."

"And that," Slade replied as they shook hands, "is, I fear, gross exaggeration."

"Oh, no, Roberto never exaggerates," Alvarez broke in. "That is, except in what he charges for his drinks. There he lets his imagination have full play."

"Roberto sells only the best," chuckled the proprietor. "The profit it is so small that I dare not drink my own wine."

"And that I don't doubt in the least," Alvarez declared heartily. "You're more sensible than I thought."

Roberto chuckled again and beckoned to a waiter. "For my *amigos*, the best," he directed. "The drinks, they are on the house, as you say in Texas. I go, but I return." He hurried off, still chuckling.

"A first rate hombre, Roberto," said Alvarez as they sat down. "Once your friend, always your friend. And I'd say, Mr. Slade, that you made a lot of friends here today. But," he added, his voice serious, "by what you've done in the past few days, I fear you have also made some bad enemies. The Faceless Riders, as those outlaws are called, will not forget."

"Quite likely they won't," Slade agreed cheerfully. "Say, this wine is a lot better than average. I'm inclined to believe Roberto when he says he sells only the best."

"Yes, only the best," nodded Alvarez. "His games are square, absolutely, and his dance floor *senoritas* are all nice girls who will not take advantage of anybody. Roberto will have no other kind."

"And I'd say he also picks them for looks," Slade observed, glancing at the dance floor, which was busy.

"Not bad," agreed Alvarez, "but let's put in our order. At my age food is more interesting than women. I would suggest the 'Steak Roberto,' Mr. Slade. It is served with a sauce that is truly delicious."

When the steak arrived, Slade quickly conceived a high opinion of Ramos Alvarez' gustatory judgment, and did full justice to its succulent size.

"And now suppose we have something to drink," suggested Randal, after the empty plates had been removed. "This wine is okay for a chaser, but it doesn't pack the wallop good old Redeye does."

"You Texans!" sighed Alvarez. "Always must you go for extremes. Why can't you be satisfied to get drunk slowly and gracefully?"

"No sense in doing anything too slowly. I never saw a graceful drunk, slow or fast," was Randal's cheerful comment. "See? Roberto thinks the same way I do.

Here he comes with a bottle of something you can really taste."

"Oh well, I've associated with you so long I guess I'm part Texan myself," said Alvarez. "Fill 'em up, *muchacho!*"

The chuckling Roberto did as directed and plunked the bottle on the table.

"It must show white from neck to bottom before you depart," he said. "Otherwise, I shall be distressed."

"Now there's an *hombre* after my own heart," declared Randal, pouring himself a second.

Despite his avowed preference for wine, Alvarez showed himself no slouch when it came to straight whiskey. Slade sipped his, and let his gaze rove over the colorful scene.

The majority of the patrons were gay, carefree young Mexicans who drank their wine and chattered together in musical Spanish interlarded with Indian expressions. There were also quite a number of young and carefree cowhands. And, Slade noted, certain individuals who wore cow country garb but who, he shrewdly suspected, could show no recent marks of rope or branding iron. This interested *El Halcon*. Evidently all sorts came to Roberto's *La Carmencita*. It was not unreasonable to believe that sooner or later the man he hoped to see might show up. He was of the opinion that signing up with Ramos Alvarez for a while was a wise move.

Newcomers drifted in from time to time, all of whom Slade noted casually. They were mostly young Mexicans similar to those already lining the bar. Then the doors opened slowly and a man entered who held his attention for a moment, being somewhat out of the ordinary. He was tall but stooped, and leaned heavily on a cane. His hair was yellow and so was his short beard. He wore heavy-lensed glasses through which he peered hesitantly. Inside the doors he paused, glancing about. Spotting Alvarez, he waves his hand and limped to the bar, favoring his left leg, his gait halting.

"That's the *Señor* Brent Dumas," volunteered Alvarez. "He owns a small ranch to the southwest of here, which he bought last year from old Don Sebastian Tolar. Pretty badly crippled, leg busted and I've a notion it wasn't set right. Rides okay, though, and is a good cowman. Incidentally, till you showed up in the section, Slade, he's the only *hombre* who's managed to bring in one of those infernal Faceless Riders. Three or four of them tried to rustle some of his cows. He caught them at it and drilled one through the back with a Winchester and sent the others hightailing. Was quite a stir when he brought the body in with a white cloth mask over the face. Said he'd just topped a rise when he saw what was going on, and cut down on the devils. Said they were out of sixgun range but just right for a rifle."

"Not bad for a man who wears glasses," Slade commented.

"Oh, he can see okay at a distance," Alvarez explained. "He's farsighted and has trouble with things close up. Something that happens to lots of folks when they're getting on in years. He isn't very young — gray in that yellow hair, if you look close. You two should get

46

together, Slade, you have something in common: the Faceless Riders will be out to get you both."

"Nice prospect!" grunted Randal. "I'd say they'd better stay apart, so they won't both fall into the same trap."

"You may have something there," Slade smiled. "But Mr. Dumas sounds interesting." He dismissed the rancher from his thoughts, however, and resumed watching the door. Alvarez recalled him to mind a moment later.

"I'm going over and have a word with Dumas," he said, rising to his feet. "He's been supplying us with beef of late; he brought in improved stock, better'n what we were formerly able to get. We run a commissary at the mine, for the majority of our workers are young fellows who don't live around close."

Randal nodded approvingly as the mine manager crossed the room to the bar.

"Al's up and coming, all right," he observed. "He's always doing something to better the conditions of his workers. Says it pays off, and I reckon it does. The real reason, though, just between you and me, is that he's a right jigger and likes to play square with everybody. I've a notion he started buying from Dumas because he's sorta new here and needed to get a start."

Slade nodded agreement; he had formed something of the same opinion of Ramos Alvarez.

The mine manager conversed with Dumas for quite a while. "Told him about the conveyor system," he announced when he returned to the table. "He thinks it's a fine idea. Said he saw one in operation, once, bringing down ore to the stamp mills from mines way up in the hills."

"Yes, they operate on the gravity principle," Slade said. "We'll employ the same procedure here, in a modified form. The tower on the north bank will be a trifle lower than that on the south bank. The loaded buckets will roll across the river on their own power and the empties be drawn back by the winding engine. There will be trips at each end of the cable, which will lower the buckets for loading and unloading."

"Sounds better all the time," chuckled Alvarez. "I've a notion it was a lucky day for me as well as for George when you decided to give this section a whirl. Let's have another drink."

"I think I'll have coffee, if you don't mind," Slade replied. "That's my favorite tipple."

"Less apt to build up a headache," Randal agreed. "I'll take a chance on the headache, though. Fill 'em up, *muchacho*."

A little later, Dumas waved good night to Alvarez and limped out, leaning heavily on his cane.

"Said he has a busy day ahead of him tomorrow and wants to get to bed early," Alvarez observed.

"Far to his place?" Slade asked.

"About five miles to his *casa*," Alvarez replied.

Randal and Alvarez began a lengthy discussion of what would be needed to construct a new ranchhouse for the Walking R, the manager making notes and jotting down figures. Slade took no part in the discussion beyond answering an occasional question put to him by Randal relative to some building point. He continued to study the room and its occupants.

The dance floor girls mingled with the patrons between numbers. One, rather taller than the average, with a really nice figure, flashing black eyes and a wealth of curly black hair, paused at the table.

"Will not the tall *senor* dance?" she asked in a soft and modulated voice. Her eyes met Slade's squarely and he thought he read a message beyond the customary "business" appeal.

"It would be a pleasure, and thank you," he said. "Nice of you to ask me."

"That's what I'm here for," she replied, demurely lowering her lashes. Slade chuckled and they made their way to the dance floor. He circled her slender waist with a long arm and when the music started, they glided onto the floor.

Walt Slade liked to dance and he could dance, and in this dark-eyed *senorita* — although he was not at all sure she was a *senorita* because of her choice of words and absence of accent — he found a fit partner.

As they circled the floor the girl spoke, very softly.

"Mr. Slade," she breathed, "you are in deadly danger."

CHAPTER
SIX

"Yes?" Slade did not appear particularly impressed.

"Yes. There are men waiting to kill you as soon as you step out the door. They are across at the corner, in the shadow of that big warehouse. When you step out they will start shooting."

Without appearing to do so, Slade studied the girl. She seemed sincere, but it could be the setting of a trap; and there is no more effective bait for a trap than a pretty woman, especially where an impressionable young man is concerned. He shot a question at her.

"How did you learn my name?"

"Everybody here knows it," she answered. "You were recognized as *El Halcon*, and Mr. Randal and Mr. Alvarez mentioned it several times."

"And how do you known those men are waiting to drygulch me?"

"Don't ask me how, but I know," she said. "We floor girls hear things, sometimes things we are not supposed to hear."

Slade nodded. "And what's your name?" he asked.

"Iris."

"Iris," he repeated, "'the rainbow.' Which is many-colored."

She seemed to get the implication, for she smiled a little, her teeth, even and white as Slade's own, flashing against her red lips.

"The rainbow is also the sign of the Covenant and signifies abiding truth," she answered.

"You're not Mexican?"

"No, I'm a Texan. I live in Boquillas, Texas, across the river."

"And why did you tell me what you did?"

"Because I don't wish to see an honest man murdered," was her retort.

Slade considered a moment. "How many men out there?" he asked.

"Two," she said, "and, as our Mexican friends say, they are *muy malo*."

"Very bad," Slade translated. "I don't doubt it. Is there a back door to this place?"

"Yes," she replied. "The hall in the back — we'll pass it in a moment — leads to it, just beyond the girls' dressing room. See, there's the entrance to the hallway. When we pass here the next time, we'll turn into it and I'll lead you to the door. Nobody will notice. If any of the girls should, they'd think nothing of it. They often meet their friends in the alley back of the *cantina*."

Slade nodded. Well, if it was a trap, here it came. He decided to take chance.

They circled the floor again, which was crowded. Apparently unnoticed, they slipped into the hallway, which was dimly lighted by a single bracket lamp at the far end. Another moment and they reached the door. Slade glanced at the lamp. Silhouetted against its light he would be a perfect target for anybody waiting outside.

Iris seemed to read his thought, for she reached up, tipped the chimney and blew out the light.

"Good girl, and smart," Slade whispered. "Can you leave the door unlocked?"

"Better than that, I'll be waiting here when you return," she promised, unlocking the door as she spoke and opening it a crack. Slade slipped through, swiftly but warily, hands close to his guns, and nothing happened. He found himself in a narrow and dark alley. The *cantina* was located but two doors from the corner. He moved to where he could see up and down the dimly lighted and deserted side street, waited a moment, peering and listening, then slipped across the street and followed the continuation of the alley to the next corner. Here, after making sure he was not observed, he crossed the main street and circled the block. With the greatest caution he approached the dark bulk of the warehouse of which Iris had spoken. Hugging the wall of the building he drew near the corner, and saw the two killers.

They stood in the shadow, gazing fixedly at the swinging doors of the *cantina* across the street. Iris had been right. There was no mistaking that watchful pose of anticipation. Slade eased forward another step, until he was less than half a dozen paces from the expectant drygulchers.

Then he called softly, "Looking for somebody, *hombres?*"

The pair whirled at the sound of his voice, stared, and went for their guns.

Slade drew and shot — left, right, left, right — the reports ringing out like thunder, lances of flame splitting the shadows. One of the killers managed to fire one wild shot, then he slumped to the ground beside his companion, whose gun had exploded as he fell.

Slade glided forward a couple of steps, guns ready for instant action; but the pair lay motionless and would undoubtedly stay that way until somebody moved them. The noise in the *cantina* had suddenly hushed. Now came a burst of yells and the pad of running feet. Slade turned and raced down the street at top speed, which he did not abate until he reached the alley. He slowed up a bit, glided across the street on which the warehouse stood and a moment later tapped softly on the *cantina* door. It opened instantly and he slipped through. Iris closed it and locked it behind him.

"Thank heaven you're safe!" she whispered. "Are you all right? Now will you believe me?"

Slade's answer was to cup his hands about her waist, lift her from the floor and kiss her on the lips, hard.

"You're a little square-shooter," he said as he dropped her on her feet, blushing and breathless. "A girl to ride the river with!"

"Thanks for the compliment," she said. I'm range bred and know how much it means. *Gracias!* Come now, and we'll slip back into the *cantina*. Everybody ran out when the shooting started, but they're coming back now. We won't be noticed."

Without attracting attention they reached their table and sat down. Men were shouting bewildered questions at one another, questions nobody seemed able to answer.

"Two hard-looking hellions, dead as doornails," said somebody. "Looks like they might have had a falling out and plugged each other. Yes, reckon that was it. Sure did a finish job of it."

Iris gazed at Slade and shuddered.

"But it was them or you," she said.

"And if it hadn't been for you, it would very likely have been me," he replied. "Here come Randal and Alvarez."

The rancher and the mine manager stared at the pair sitting composedly at the table. Then old George relieved his surcharged feelings with an explosive, "Well, I'll be d-d —" remembered there was a lady present and finished lamely — "d-doggoned!"

"What's all the excitement about?" Slade asked mildly. "Sit down and have some coffee — we were just going to have a cup. Or would you prefer wine, Iris?"

"I like coffee," she replied. "I don't drink much wine."

"To which your complexion attests," Slade said. However, he ordered a bottle, knowing it was the customary thing to do and would provide her with an excuse to skip a couple of numbers on the floor.

"It won't go to waste," Alvarez promised blithely. He continued to stare at Slade, shaking his head from time to time. Randal appeared equally bewildered. Slade smiled tantalizingly and kept silent for a few more

54

minutes. Then he told them of the shooting and the events leading up to it, in detail.

"Ma'am," old George said heavily, "I already owe this carcass of mine to Slade, but I reckon you've got a sort of second mortgage on it. But how come a girl like you is floor dancing in a *cantina*?"

Iris shrugged daintily. "A girl must live," she replied. "My father and mother are both dead and I live with a widowed aunt, across the river, and Roberto is a good man to work for. He treats his girls right."

"That I don't doubt," said Alvarez. "But I'd appreciate it if you could find it convenient to drop in at my office tomorrow afternoon. I'd have been quite peeved if I'd passed on before getting a chance to see my new conveyor system working. Don't you think it would be a good idea for her to do so, Slade?"

"I do," the Ranger replied positively. "You'll do as Mr. Alvarez requests, Iris?"

"Yes, if you wish me to," the girl promised.

"I do wish you to," he said.

When Iris went back to the floor, Alvarez observed: "Not much doubt but we would have all three gotten it if we'd stepped out that door together. Yes, we're all in her debt. I'll put her to work in the office at twice whatever she makes here."

"A nice thing you're doing, Mr. Alvarez," Slade said. "I think it is a very good idea to get her out of the *cantina*. No telling who may have noticed us together, and somebody might have tumbled to what went on. I also think it would be a good idea to keep a close eye on her for a while. If that outfit of hellions should guess the part she played, I wouldn't put it past them to try and even up the score."

"I'll keep an eye on her," Alvarez promised grimly. "I haven't packed a gun for quite a while, but I'm going to start again tomorrow. Now, George, I believe we've got everything lined up, haven't we? If so, suppose we go to bed. You fellows come along to my place — plenty of room. I'm a bachelor, Slade, and have a big *casa* with more room than I need, so it'll be a pleasure to put you both up. And you'll be riding to Marathon day after tomorrow to get in touch with the Laredo people? Fine! I'll have the authority you need ready for you at the office tomorrow. And by the way, suppose you stop 'mistering' me. When three men just miss taking the big jump together, I figure they should dispense with all formalities. Call me Al, same as George does."

"Okay, Al," Slade smiled, adding, "and I believe you know my first name."

"That's right, Walt," Alvarez chuckled. "Let's go!"

All three turned to wave good night to Iris on the dance floor, who waved back, her eyes fixed on Slade's face. A thought struck Alvarez.

"Just a minute," he told his companions. "I want to speak with Roberto." He drew the owner aside and conversed earnestly for a moment. Roberto nodded emphatically.

"Thought it would be a good idea to put a bug in his ear," he said when he rejoined the others. "He's taking Iris to his place tonight after she finishes work. She'll be safe there. His *senora* weighs two hundred and can dot a lizard's eye with a sixgun at thirty paces. And she likes to shoot."

"Looks like *Senora* Roberto would make a valuable ally," Slade chuckled.

"She would," agreed Alvarez, "and besides, she's one of the sweetest and most charming women you ever met. She's just as nice as Roberto, and that's saying plenty. Incidentally, don't be fooled by Roberto's fat; I've seen him jump three feet off the floor, flat-footed, and kick a man in the jaw."

"Yep, he can be plenty salty when he needs to be," nodded Randal. "Let's go."

Before going to bed in a very comfortable room, Slade cleaned and oiled his guns, meanwhile pondering the attempted drygulching. Looked very much like he had been spotted, and by Sosna himself. He did not think that the bodies of the Faceless Riders in the thicket had been discovered so soon, Slade being credited with their demise. Either Sosna himself had spotted him or had received word that *El Halcon* was in the section. Either of which meant that the outlaw leader was somewhere close at hand.

Well, that was all to the good, although it undoubtedly laid him open to grave personal danger. He had come to the Big Bend in search of Veck Sosna, and the sooner he found him the better. But he had to admit there was a good chance that the shrewd and daring outlaw might do the "finding." An eventuality which must be seriously considered and guarded against if he hoped to stay in the land of the living.

Well, Sosna had had quite a few tries at him and had failed up each time, so *El Halcon* was not particularly perturbed over the chance of more of a similar nature. He had been assigned the chore of bringing Veck Sosna to justice and that's what he intended to do. He went to sleep with a tranquil mind.

CHAPTER
SEVEN

When Slade and George Randal rode out of Boquillas shortly after noon the following day, they headed a caravan. Three huge freight wagons, loaded to capacity with building materials, rolled northward. Alvarez had pulled a crew of his own expert carpenters from the mine to go along and expedite the ranchhouse construction. He had also insisted that half a dozen of his best mine guards accompany the wagons.

"I'm taking no chances with those hellions," he said. "They might take it into their ornery heads to try another drygulching. So if they come looking for trouble, we'll give it to them until it curls their whiskers. Never mind the argument, I know what I'm doing. Think I want something to happen to Slade before he gets that conveyor system working? You see I have a selfish interest in the matter. Be seeing you both. Slade, you're all set to get whatever is needed sifting sand out of Laredo."

Randal chuckled as the wagons rumbled along the trail. "Al not only manages the mine, he owns about half of it," he observed. "Owns a mighty big ranch, too, and has a finger in some other pies. He's a rich man, but you'd never think it the way he talks and acts. Just one of the boys."

"As a gentleman, a Spanish-Mexican of the old school is hard to equal," Slade replied. "If he'd been born about four hundred years earlier, the chances are he'd have a band of Conquistadores mavericking into the wilderness to see what was over the next hilltop. Those old jiggers had plenty of sand in their craws, and he'd fit right into that category."

They reached the site of the Walking R *casa* without incident and found that, in pursuance of Randal's orders, the big barn had been fitted up as temporary living quarters. There was plenty of room for all and everybody was made comfortable. Felipe, his leg much better, threw together a surrounding commensurate to the occasion.

Old George chortled loud and long as he and Slade walked about the yard together.

"They're still trying to figure why those two hellions they found on the street corner gunned each other, I reckon," he said. "Everybody seemed to agree that they did for each other, but why? Nobody seemed to know them or where they came from."

"Glad it turned out that way," Slade replied. "I gathered that the *alcade* was quite put out about it. Would appear he doesn't look kindly on shootings in the town he's mayor of."

"Yep, takes his job seriously," Randal agreed. "Well, tomorrow we'll head to Marathon to attend to our chores there. I think we'll take three or four of the boys along, just in case. They're not needed here with those

60

carpenters on the job under Alvarez' instructions to do everything hunkydory. Okay with you?"

"Yes," Slade replied. "The sooner the better. Alvarez is itching to see that conveyor system in operation; he'll be like a kid with a new toy. I don't want to hold him up."

"Right," nodded Randal, "tomorrow morning, early, we'll trail our twine."

That night Walt Slade played a hunch. He had elected to sleep in the newly prepared barn quarters despite Randal's protests that the bunkhouse would be more comfortable.

"Barn's plenty good enough," he replied cheerfully. "I'll pound my ear there. I've pounded it in a lot worse places."

Such was his announced intention to sleep in the barn. But he didn't. Instead, he spread his blanket beneath a tree that grew close to the trail which ran past the ranch-house yard and went to sleep peacefully, knowing that any unusual sound would instantly awaken him.

A sound unusual for that lonely trail at that time of night did awaken him in the dark hour before the dawn: the muffled beat of horses' hoofs on the dusty surface. Instantly he was sitting up, alert, watchful. The low moon cast a wan light across the track, simmering each grain of dust, tracing a web of shadows where tree branches filtered the beams.

The sound steadily grew, coming from the south. Slade sat in the gloom beneath the tree, waiting.

There was something stealthy about that slow advance, as if the unseen riders were peering cautiously and expectantly into the receding wall of the shadows. Slade could vision their heads thrust forward, their bridle hands tense.

The tempo of the beats was not that which would be expected from the mounts of a bunch of cowhands heading home after an evening in Boquillas. It was neither fast nor slow; rather cautious but purposeful. Slade sat waiting, his eyes fixed on the point where the trail curved around a bristle of growth.

At the apex of the curve, shapes materialized, grotesque, distorted in the faint light, growing larger, taking on form, becoming mounted men. Slade counted six altogether. He sat relaxed in his blankets, waiting, certain now that his hunch had been a straight one. The whitish blur that were faces turned in his direction, held. He could not make out features, but one of the ghostly riders of the night appeared much taller than the others.

He watched them drift past, saw the faces turn to the front. A few minutes after receding from the site of the burned ranchhouse, the tempo of the hoofbeats quickened, took on a carefree note, as of something satisfactorily accomplished, an anxiety relieved. They drummed away into the distance. Slade fished out the makin's and rolled and lighted a cigarette.

"It was them, all right, the Faceless Riders, or some of them, and the tall one could very well be Sosna himself," he told the glowing tip. "They learned or figured out that I'd ride to Marathon today and aimed to get ahead of me. Well, that's okay, now that I *know* they're ahead of me."

Finishing his smoke, he carefully pinched out the butt, curled up again and slept soundly till daylight.

After breakfast, Slade and Randal and four of Randal's most trusted and competent hands rode north. They passed the Chisos, flaming with many-colored splendor in the sunlight, and continued to Persimmon Gap, which they reached without incident. Slade rode watchful and alert, although he didn't really expect any trouble on the trail. Veck Sosna had learned from experience the futility of trying to ambush *El Halcon*. Whatever he had in mind was something more subtle and consequently more deadly than a drygulching that might well prove abortive with disastrous results to himself. Slade believed that whatever the outlaw leader planned would be put into effect after they reached Marathon. What it might be he had not the slightest notion, and so he was prepared for anything. Sosna's cunning and farsighted mind would doubtless evolve something out of the ordinary.

Which, he was forced to admit, gave him no little cause for concern; Veck Sosna's genius for the unexpected was not to be lightly discounted. But his inordinate vanity and his flair for the spectacular might, Slade believed, be his ultimate downfall. Anyhow, he hoped so.

In the mouth of the gap, Slade turned in his saddle to gaze at the rugged grandeur and weird beauty of the view that was the Big Bend. His spirit was uplifted by the stupendous scene that man could never spoil and he faced to the front with renewed confidence.

They traversed the wild and desolate pass, a suspension bridge in the clouds, with no untoward happening. Cupola peak and the twin peaks of Dove Mountain came into view; a little farther on, Yellow Horse Peak on the right, Santiago Peak on the left, with the mighty loom of the Deleware Mountains to the northwest and the Glass Mountains almost due north, beyond Marathon. They crossed Maravillas Creek and after thirty more miles of steady riding reached Marathon, treeless, arid, mountain-bound. The town was the supply center for a vast ranching country extending almost across the six thousand square miles of Brewster County, covering the Big Bend. Marathon boasted many unpainted adobes and other and more substantial buildings.

It had been a long ride and a hard one. The lovely blue dusk was sifting down from the mountains like impalpable dust and lights were beginning to twinkle when they entered the town, the tired horses plodding, their riders anxious for food and other things.

"Too late to do anything tonight," Randal observed to Slade. "I know a place where we can get rooms. The boys call it the Astor House, but I've a notion it falls a mite short of the one in New York I've read about. Sign hanging out front used to have a name on it, but that's faded away long ago. Oh, by the way, there's something I forgot to tell you. Sort of slipped my mind, so many other things to think about. Remember that crippled rancher Alvarez pointed out to us?"

64

Slade nodded. "Dumas, I believe Alvarez said his name was."

"That's right, Brent Dumas. Well, when Al and I were checking over the stuff I ordered before we left town, Dumas hobbled in. Said he'd looked over the carcasses of those two sidewinders you did for. Said he was just about sure for certain they were part of the bunch that tried to wideloop his cows. You'll rec'lect he killed one and brought in the body, with a white mask over the face."

"Wonder how he came to recognize them, if they were masked when he saw them after his cows?" Slade commented.

"'Pears he's got good eyes for distance seeing," Randal replied. "I believe Al mentioned that the other night. He said that one of them had one shoulder higher than the other and that the other one had a crooked neck. That sort of tallied with the carcasses I gather. He's positive they were part of the Faceless Riders."

"Interesting," Slade observed. "Sort of corroborates what we believe."

"That's right," agreed Randal. "Although it 'pears those two didn't have any white masks in their pockets like the three we had the rukus with in the thicket did."

"Quite likely they don't always carry them," Slade remarked. "I expect they only pack them along when they expect to make a raid."

"Chances are you're right," Randal agreed. "Well, here's a stable that'll take care of the cayuses. We'll sign up for rooms in the hotel and rustle something to eat. I'm starved."

The Astor House was not much to look at, but the rooms were clean and comfortable. Slade and his companions signed up for quarters and then repaired to a nearby saloon which Randal said served good chuck.

"Likker's not bad, either," he observed after a couple of brimming glasses.

"Always like something for my chuck to splash into," he explained as he downed the second glass. "Now I'm all set to chaw on something." Which he proceeded to do without delay and with gusto.

The saloon, the First Chance, was crowded and lively. Most of the patrons were cowhands from the spreads flowing across the far-flung acres of the Big Bend. And most of them were young, gay, reckless, living for today and to hell with tomorrow. A sprinkling of grizzle-heads among them were a bit more composed, but not much; the Texas Big Bend country keeps men young in heart if not in years.

All of which Slade noticed with interest and pleasure. He felt his pulses quicken, as they always did where life geysered up in many-colored phases, raw, hearty, full of energy. He enjoyed the setting and was glad to be a part of it, but he was beset by an undercurrent of very serious thought. He was convinced that Veck Sosna and his men were somewhere in Marathon, doubtless cooking up deviltry of one sort or another. It was up to him to, if possible, anticipate its nature and try to forestall it. And if that failed, to be ready for and counteract whatever the cunning hellion had in mind.

After eating, the Walking R hands headed for the bar and soon were as hilarious as the rest. Slade bit back a grin as he watched old George grow restless. Finally the owner could stand it no longer.

"Figure I'd better get over there and keep an eye on the boys," he said apologetically. Slade nodded sober assent, but with a dancing light in the depths of his gray eyes. Yes, the Big Bend country kept men young.

"I'll join you after a while," he told the rancher. "Feel like taking it easy here for a bit longer."

Randal nodded. Slade sat on at the table, watching the door. He did not expect to see Sosna enter, but he thought the outlaw leader might send somebody to give the place a once-over. And very likely, he believed, the spy would betray his mission by too intently searching the room when he entered, and fixing his gaze, if only momentarily, on the man he sought.

But if Sosna did dispatch one of his men to the First Chance, the emissary was too shrewd to give anything away. Slade watched people come and go and saw nothing to cause him to suspect that one of those who entered and departed might be connected with the Faceless Riders.

Finally he gave it up and joined Randal at the bar. But he was too preoccupied to really take part in the hilarity, and when, around midnight, Randal announced that he'd had enough and was going to bed, Slade decided to do likewise.

The room, toward the back of the hotel, on the second floor, was restful after the turmoil in the saloon. The town's turbulent night life was muted to a murmur. A tall tree, one of the few in the section, grew not far from the window and light filtered by the branches traced graceful and soothing patterns of shadow on floor and walls. Slade undressed and stretched out, enjoying relaxing comfortably before drifting off to sleep.

CHAPTER
EIGHT

Slade was awakened by a sharp crack followed by a solid thud. He was out of bed and on his feet in a single ripple of motion. Before him loomed a man, and on the floor a flower of fire hissed and sputtered.

Just in time he saw the sparkle of the lunging knife. He slewed sideways and the blade grained the flesh over his ribs. He caught the fellow's wrist before he could repeat the stroke and held on despite the other's struggles to break free. Then a hand closed on his throat in a throttling grip. He struck out with his free hand, but the fellow ducked his face against his chest and took the blows on the top of his head.

Slade dared not let go his opponent's wrist. To do so would be to invite the death stroke of the keen blade. And the grip on his throat stopped his breath. His lungs swelled to bursting. Red flashes stormed before his eyes. His strength was draining away.

And on the floor the flower of fire hissed like an angry serpent a thousand times more deadly.

Back and forth the battlers swayed in a furious death grapple. The fellow fought desperately to win free, but could not. But neither could the Ranger, and at any instant the bundle of capped and fused dynamite would let go and blow them both into eternity.

They whirled around, Slade with his back to the window. With all his remaining strength he hurled himself backward to the floor. His opponent flew over him as Slade's leg, rigid as a bar of steel, shot up to catch him in the midriff. His grip was torn loose from the Ranger's throat, and as Slade let go his wrist he crashed through the window, taking frame and glass with him in splintered ruin. Slade scrambled to his feet, scooped up the bundle of dynamite with the fire licking the cap and hurled it through the window. Trailing sparks, it whizzed between the tree branches. One deflected it and it hit the ground several yards distant and exploded with a thundering roar.

Slade was slammed clean across the room by the concussion, bringing up against the door with a crash, the breath knocked out of his body. Gasping, he sagged against the wall, dimly conscious that a tinkle of falling glass followed the bellow of the explosion. Every window on that side of the hotel was shattered, as were those of nearby buildings.

For an instant there was utter stillness, then the silence was shattered by a veritable volcano blast of yells, screams, shouts and curses. Slade staggered to the frameless window and peered out. Moonlight seeping between the tree branches showed a smoking crater hollowed in the earth.

It showed something else: a stout branch running parallel to the window, a little below and but a few feet distant, was snapped off short. Slade gazed at the broken limb and understood.

"Hellion climbed the tree and inched out along the branch till he was opposite the window," he muttered. "Leaned over to ease the dynamite into the room. Limb busted and threw him through the window. Trying to save himself, he dropped the dynamite. A miracle it didn't cut loose when it hit the floor. Yes, that was it. As the Yaquis would say, my 'spirit' sure looked my way tonight!"

Leaving the window, Slade threw on his clothes at top speed. He buckled on his guns and opened the door.

A man came hop-skipping down the hall, one boot on, one off, his hair fairly bristling on his head.

"Earthquake!" he screeched. "Couldn't have been nothin' else. Lemme outa here!" He whizzed past and down the steps like a high-powered rifle bullet. Others came after him, all cursing and yelling. The combined uproar dwarfed the explosion.

Slade remained in the doorway and let them pass; to do otherwise would have been like bucking a cow stampede head-on. When the hall was clear again, he closed the door and sauntered down the stairs.

The lobby was filled with men in all stages of undress. There were also quite a few scantily clad dance floor girls. The air quivered to questions volleyed at nobody in particular and not expecting an answer.

Slade spotted George Randal, shirtless, and approached him.

"What in blazes was it? Have you any notion?" demanded the rancher. "Sounded like the whole blasted town blew up."

"Talk to you later," Slade replied. "Let's go outside for a look around."

When they approached the back of the building, they found a crowd gathering around the hole in the ground, talking excitedly, gesturing. Suddenly somebody let out a yell: "Holy Pete! Here's a leg!"

"And here's an arm!" another voice howled. "What in the blankety-blank-blank?"

"Can't you figure it?" a third voice chimed in. "Some loco prospector was packing a supply of dynamite for his claim out in the hills somewhere. Drunk, I reckon. Fell down or bumped into the tree and the powder cut loose. Don't look like there's enough left of him for a buryin'."

The crowd, which was constantly augmented by new arrivals, appeared ready to accept the explanation, which was wholly satisfactory to Slade. He took Randal by the arm, led him aside and told him what really happened.

The rancher swore viciously, his eyes snapping. "So the devils are after you for fair, eh?" he growled. A worried look spread over his face.

"Son," he said, "I'm afraid I'm to blame for this trouble. If you hadn't hauled me out of that burning shack and then tangled with the hellions on the trail, on my account, they wouldn't be on the prod against you."

"Don't let that bother you," Slade reassured him. "Later I'll tell you why. Anyhow, they haven't had any luck so far, and I figure maybe I'll keep on getting the breaks. Come on and let's get inside. You'll catch your death of cold mavericking around without your shirt. Then we'll try and rustle a cup of hot coffee. Do us both good. Getting close to daylight and sleep's out for the rest of the night, what little's left of it. Come on."

Randal donned his shirt and they repaired to the First Chance for the coffee and some breakfast. The place was crowded with men excitedly discussing the explosion, which apparently had roused the whole town. Slade and the rancher found a vacant table and gave their orders to a waiter who looked like he could use some sleep.

"Ain't been so much excitement since the Faceless Riders held up Cartwright's Saloon and shot him," remarked Randal. "Reckon folks would be even a mite more excited if they knew the truth of what happened. Guess we'd better keep that under our hats, though. Right?"

"Yes, I think it would be best," Slade replied. "I don't want to be asked a lot of questions I don't care to answer."

Randal nodded and glanced toward the door. "Here comes Sheriff Dobson," he exclaimed. "I want you to meet him. He's okay and we've been mighty good friends for a lot of years. Fact is, he was my range boss once, before he got into politics and got elected." He waved his hand to the peace officer and beckoned.

The sheriff was a big raw-boned, loose-joineed man in range clothes, with graying hair and mustache. His legs were slightly bowed, his arms extremely long, and his dangling hands reminded Slade of spear points. His eyes widened slightly as they rested on Slade's face, but otherwise his weatherbeaten countenance was impassive as a deal board.

"Cain," said Randal as he drew near, "I want you to know Walt Slade, a pertickler *amigo* of mine. I'm sorta beholden to him for being alive, which I reckon means something. Slade, this is Sheriff Cain Dobson."

"Means something to me, I reckon," said the sheriff as he shook hands. "I'd hate not having the chance to point you out to folks as a prime example of a misspent life. Glad to know you, Slade, even though I do find you in bad company. Drop in and see me when you get a chance. George can tell you where my branch office is. I have a deputy stationed here. This pueblo is a trouble spot."

Slade already knew where the office was, but he merely said, "Thank you, Sheriff, I'll do that before we head back for the spread tomorrow morning."

The sheriff nodded. "Be seeing you, George," he said, and strolled to the bar.

"Going to tell him?" Randal asked.

"Yes, I think I shall," Slade replied. "He should know what is going on, and I've a notion he can keep a tight latigo on his jaw."

"He can," agreed Randal. "He's all right, but I'm scared those blasted Faceless Riders are a mite too much for him. If he could just lock horns with the hellions my money would be on him. But they always seem a jump ahead of him."

"A jump ahead of everybody," Slade said morosely, with a meaning that was lost on the rancher. "Well, here comes our sleep walking waiter with the coffee. It's welcome."

After plenty of coffee, steaming hot, and a hearty breakfast both felt in a more cheerful frame of mind.

"I'm heading for the telegraph office. It should be open by now," Slade announced. "Want to start things moving for Alvarez."

"And I'm going to see if I can tie onto a chair or two and a table," said Randal. "Got to start from scratch to furnish the new *casa*. Will need a freight wagon load of stuff, maybe two. I'll meet you here about noon."

At the telegraph office, *El Halcon* immediately got busy. Messages clicked back and forth over the wires — question and answer, calculation and estimate. Slade knew exactly what was needed and with an engineer's knowledge was able to provide the construction company's representative with all necessary physical data relative to the terrain, and the problems that would be met and their solution. In less than two hours the transaction was completed.

The final message read: WILL BE READY TO START WORK BY THE MIDDLE OF NEXT WEEK, Slade left the office with the satisfaction of a chore well done.

His next visit was to the sheriff's office, where he found Cain Dobson in. After closing the door and making sure the curtains were drawn, the sheriff shook hands warmly.

"Well, how's the notorious outlaw today?" he asked.

"Fine as frog hair, only I'm afraid he'll have to take a back seat for the present," Slade replied. "Right now, you've a genuine died in-the-wool-and-a-yard-wide specimen on your hands."

"You mean those blasted Faceless Riders, eh?" growled the sheriff.

"I mean the man who heads the Faceless Riders," Slade corrected. "He's in a class by himself, and he isn't a man, he's a devil. I'll tell you about him."

In detail, he gave Dobson an account of his contacts with Veck Sosna in the Canadian River Valley country and elsewhere, including tracking the owlhoot to his hidden sanctuary in the Valley of Tears, and Sosna's subsequent escape.

"Thought I had him that time, but he grabbed a freight train at the last minute and gave me the slip," Slade concluded. "I've been tracking him, off and on, for the past two years and finally I've caught up with him to the extent of knowing where he's operating, which is here in the Big Bend country. I followed him to east Texas, into the Big Thicket section, to Beaumont, down to the Gulf Coast. And there I lost the trail and it took me a long time to pick it up again. Up in the Panhandle, a fellow once said that wherever Sosna went he left a trail of skeletons behind him. Which was and is true. That's how I finally picked up the trail again, following the track of a lot of seemingly senseless killings; killings just for the pleasure of killings, which is Sosna's way. Yes, he's a devil and takes pleasure from sadistic cruelty. Which, I believe and hope, will finally get him his comeuppance."

"And that's why you're here, eh?" remarked Dobson.

"Yes, that's why I'm here, but McNelty didn't send me here, Slade replied. "Sosna is in the nature of unfinished business, which Captain Jim knows, of course, so he won't object to this little sideways sashay of mine. Sosna is a challenge to the Rangers."

"I sure haven't had any luck with him," grunted Dobbs. "This is the first time I've even got a notion as to who he is."

"He's shrewd, salty, utterly fearless and utterly ruthless," Slade said. "Last night was a fair example of how he works. The fact that he might well kill a dozen innocent people meant nothing to him just so long as he achieved his objective, to get me out of his way."

"Last night? What do you mean?"

Slade regaled him with an explanation of the true nature of the dynamite explosion. Dobson swore.

"I'm inclined to agree with you. He ain't a man, he's a devil," the sheriff declared. "Everybody thinks it was just some fool prospector packing dynamite for his claim up in the hills. I did a mite of scouting around this morning and learned that a feller did buy half a dozen sticks yesterday at one of the general stores. Storekeeper said he didn't look like a desert rat, but you never can tell about those jiggers, so he didn't pay him any mind. Said he was sort of tall and wore cowhand clothes, which is out of the ordinary for a prospector or miner."

Slade nodded, not at all surprised. "It was a nicely planned try, and unusual," he observed. "Just the mischance of that tree branch breaking and pitching him into the room kept it from working. Sort of gave me the creeps, when I had time to think about it."

"I don't wonder," agreed Dobson. "Me, I'd still be shaking like a dog sitting on a cactus spine. Sometimes I think you haven't any nerves at all."

"It didn't work, and that's all that counts," Slade said cheerfully. "Now I'm busy wondering what will be his next move."

"Think he might try it again tonight?" asked the sheriff.

"Unlikely, I'd say, but you never can tell about Sosna. You can't measure his notions with a conventional yardstick. Look for the unexpected where he's concerned and you'll have a better chance of being right."

"You'll get him, of that I haven't any doubt, but just the same you'd better keep your eyes skinned," said Dobson. "You've not revealed your Ranger connections, I suppose?"

"No," Slade replied. "I believe, though of course I could be wrong, that Sosna has never learned I'm a Ranger. I think he just looks on me as another owlhoot trying to horn in on his preserves. And he's out to keep me from doing it. Well, if your number isn't up, not even Veck Sosna can put it up."

"That way of thinking sort of says it doesn't matter what we do or don't do, won't count anyhow," commented the sheriff.

"Wrong!" Slade answered. "It is for us to do everything in our power to prevent it being put up, and when things get beyond us, I believe that very likely

Something will reach down and take a hand. That is if we are in the right and it's to our best interests. We have our part of the chore to do and shouldn't ask help with something we can take care of ourselves."

"And that," the sheriff said sententiously, "is Faith."

"Without which life wouldn't be worth living," Slade said, his cold eyes suddenly all kindness. Sheriff Cain Dobson nodded silent agreement.

CHAPTER
NINE

After leaving the sheriff's office, Slade wandered
around for a while, studying faces, listening to
fragments of conversation. Three years and more had
passed since a previous visit to Marathon, but so far as
he could see, the town hadn't changed much. It was
still dry, dusty, and bustling. Cow ponies stood at the
long hitchracks, their riders high-heeling along the
sidewalks and crowding the saloons. Desert rats and hill
prospectors plodded past, often driving laden burrows.
They wore patched and faded overalls and blue shirts,
floppy hats and scuffed boots, but their eyes were
dream-filled. Slade wondered if such as these hadn't
read a-right the riddle of life and had found peace and
contentment.

Sleeping under the stars, working under the sun,
close to nature, they had absorbed the quiet confidence
of the mountains and the deserts that were their home.
All hoped to make the big strike some day, but Slade
shrewdly suspected that those who did — and they
were not too few — seldom changed their mode of
living. They still looked over the next hilltop, and went
to find out what was there. The strivings, the sorrows

and the barren achievements of the world passed them by.

El Halcon sighed. It was destined that such a life was not for him. But our Lord walked the ways of the world to right its wrongs. The sigh ended in a smile.

Aside from a certain philosophic satisfaction achieved, the stroll proved barren of results. If Sosna was still in town he was keeping under cover. Slade made his way to the First Chance, where he found Randal waiting.

"Time to eat," said the rancher. "I've been busy as a packrat in a jewelry store. Got everything pretty well attended to, though. How about you?"

"I'm all set," Slade replied. "Alvarez will be watching his conveyor system take shape this time next week."

"Then what do you say we head for home?" Randal suggested. "We'll be late getting in, but the horses are rested and I don't see any sense in loafing around here all afternoon and tonight. The boys are all here in the saloon and we can start as soon as we eat."

"Okay by me," Slade replied, slipping the coffee the waiter had brought. Personally he thought the move might throw Sosna off guard, if he was still hanging around somewhere near, waiting for night. Which Slade felt was not beyond the realm of possibility. Randal had, the previous evening, mentioned remaining in Marathon a second night and Sosna, apparently able to learn everything, had doubtless heard of the rancher's expressed intentions. Immediate departure might, for once, get the jump on the crafty hellion.

An hour later, Slade and his companions left Marathon. They rode steadily at a good pace, but it was midnight before they reached the Walking R. After caring for their horses, dog-tired, they tumbled into bed and slept till late morning.

It was surprising the amount of work Alvarez' carpenters had accomplished during their absence. Wall beams were up, plates and slips set, king posts and ridge pole in place, and a portion of the rafters.

"Those jiggers sure know their business," Randal said to Slade.

"Yes, they certainly do," the Ranger agreed. "And they work like beavers. You'll have your *casa* ready to move in by the time your furnishings arrive."

"I don't doubt it," Randal conceded. "Yep, they're okay, and they're earning a nice bonus, if they only knew it. The barn is all right for sleeping for a while, but old bones need a comfortable bed. You'll find out, if you last that long."

"Here's hoping," Slade laughed. Randal also laughed and turned to Jeff Carter, his range boss, who had joined them.

"Anything happen while we were gone?" he asked.

"Nope, nothing much," replied Carter. "Night before last, along toward daylight, some fellers rode past likerty-split. The wind was blowing cold and I'd got up to close a window. There were five of them and they sure were sifting sand."

Slade's eyes grew thoughtful. Three nights before, six men had ridden north. The following night, according to Carter, five had ridden south. He wondered if the five could have been Sosna and four of his hellions, the sixth man having been left in Marathon to attend to the dynamiting chore. Not beyond the realm of possibility, but why the quick return of the outlaw leader and some of his followers? Didn't seem to make sense. But then, nothing Sosna did ever seemed to make sense on the surface. And Sosna never did anything without a reason. This time what could the reason be? Slade didn't know, but he did know that there was nothing to be gained by puzzling over the matter. Chances were he'd learn soon enough, and that it would be something unpleasant. He dismissed the question for the time being.

"Slade," Randal suddenly said, "everything 'pears to be under control here and the boys will be busy all day helping the carpenters. So what you say we take a little ride? I'd like to look things over out on the range, and show you the spread. Okay?"

"I'll be glad to," Slade answered.

"Sky's sorta gray, but I don't figure it'll rain," Randal commented as they got the rigs on their horses. "A bit cooler with the sun behind the clouds."

"Yes, a nice day for a ride," Slade agreed.

Compared to the vast spreads of the Panhandle country, the Walking R was small, but it was plenty big, embracing as it did the entire valley. Randal pointed out salient features as they rode east not far from the northern hill slopes, and Slade quickly decided that the holding was a good one. The grass was bountiful. There were thickets and groves, and the hills were scored by canyons and gorges which provided shelter from the sun and the storms.

"Trails through those hills, too, for those who know them," Randal replied to his comment. "We have to keep our eyes skinned for wideloopers. The tracks to the south lead to Mexico, where there's always a market for wet cows. Over to the east, where we're heading, an old smuggler trail runs up the slope through thick brush and that one's always been a favorite with rustlers. It curves around to the south, and there are off-shoots the hellions can slide into and make it hard to run 'em down. I've lost quite a few head that way. But usually we have the range pretty well patrolled. That's one reason I wanted to ride over this way today; been so busy for the past few days that range riding has been sorta neglected."

Slade eyed the silver flash of a distant stream. "Looks like you've got better than average water for this section," he commented.

"That's right," said Randal. "Two creeks run clean across the spread. They come from under cliffs in canyons over here to the north and finally dive into holes in the ground in canyons down to the south."

The Ranger nodded. "There is a vast subterranean water flow under all this section of Texas. Folks will sooner or later come to understand and realize its value," he said. "Some day dry pastures in this end of the state will be watered by artesian wells that will tap the underground streams and lakes."

"Those are the wells that shoot water up into the air, ain't they?" asked Randal.

"Yes," Slade replied. "The underground water is subject to pressure much the same as an oil pool is often depressed by an accumulation of gas and bursts forth with great force when the cap rock is drilled through."

Slade's prophecy was to later be fulfilled.

After a while they splashed their horses through the first of the creeks, quite a sizeable stream, and rode on toward the loom of the eastern mountains. Slade noted with appreciation the condition of the cows grazing on the lush grass.

"See you're improving your stock," he remarked.

"Yep," replied Randal. "Folks are demanding better beef than old mossy-horns can supply. I've been doing a lot of crossing and am getting good results. It pays off."

Finally, after several hours of riding, they were in the shadow of the eastern slopes, which were steep and brush-grown. Here they turned south and rode parallel to the hills.

"After a bit, we'll circle around and head for home," Randal said as they neared the center of the valley. "Look up there to your left, about a quarter of a mile ahead."

Following his pointing finger, Slade saw what appeared to be a depression in the growth that wound crookedly up the slope to level off on what was evidently a broad bench nearly half a mile up from the valley floor.

"That's the smuggler trail I was telling you about," Randal announced. "The one that slides through a pass and runs straight to the Rio Grande. Say, what you looking at?"

El Halcon's gaze was not directed at the depression which marked the smuggler trail. His attention was fixed on something almost due west. Randal also quickly noted it.

"What the devil!" he sputtered. "That's a herd moving this way, moving fast, too."

Slade was studying the distant herd with his hawk's eyes, estimating the number of cows, checking the number of riders.

"Yes," he said, "coming fast. Two hundred head or more. Are any of your boys out on the range this afternoon?"

"Heck, no," replied Randal. "I ordered 'em all to stay and help the carpenters."

"Any other outfit use your range?"

"No," Randal answered. "What the devil does it mean?"

"It means," Slade replied dryly, "that some of the wide-loopers you were talking about are out to glom onto a little purloined beef."

Randal let out a yelp of rage and turned his horse. "I'll put a stop to that," he growled. "I'm going to —"

But Slade instantly caught his bit iron and jerked the horse back.

"You're going to stay right here," he said with finality. "There are seven riders shoving those cows; we wouldn't have a chance in the open. Hold it, this will take a mite of thinking out. Move over closer to the brush. I'm pretty sure they can't see us against it; this gray sky's getting darker all the time. Okay, this will do."

Ignoring the fuming rancher, he studied their immediate surroundings, his gaze traveling ahead.

"That trail up the slope, the one you called an old smuggler trail, do you figure they're heading for that?"

"Sure they are," declared Randal. "It's the only one over in this direction, and the straightest shoot to Mexico."

"Okay," Slade said. "We'll make for that trail and get there ahead of them. I'd say the brush is tall enough to hide a man on horseback. Come on and we'll try to locate a spot where the odds won't all be against us. With luck, we may be able to give those cow lifting gents a mite of a surprise."

They drifted their horses close to the growth until they reached the beginning of the trail. As Slade expected, the brush was so tall and thick and flanked the trail so closely, they were invisible to the rustlers shoving the herd along in the distance.

The trail wound up and up, finally leveling off on a wide bench. Sheltered from the rain as it was, the dust was deep and their horses' irons made but a soft clumping sound and each footfall raised spurts that grayed the air.

"Those cows will set it fogging," Slade observed. "Maybe the better for us, but won't make for accurate shooting, and we can't afford to do much missing. Here's hoping we'll find the right kind of a hole-up spot soon. Dark isn't far off."

A few miles along the bench they found it, a straight stretch with a gentle downgrade.

"This will be fine," Slade said. "We'll hole up a couple of hundred yards down the straightaway. The cows will be blowing after the climb, but they'll speed up a bit here, which will be to our advantage. Okay, into the brush we go. Tie your cayuse well back from the trail, if he won't stand. Don't want to take chances on the critters getting nicked by a stray slug. This'll be far enough."

Slade nodded and dropped the split reins to the ground, knowing that Shadow would not move. He drew his Winchester from the saddle boot and led the way back to the trail. Behind a fringe of growth they took up their stand. Slade glanced at Randal's old Smith, drew one of his Colts and passed it to the rancher.

"Shoot with both of them as fast as you can," he directed. "I'm using my rifle to start with. Shoot fast and yell as loud as you can. If we make enough racket maybe they won't tumble to the fact that there are only two of us. We've got to make them think the whole Walking R outfit is holed up here waiting for them. The herd will be ahead of them and that should add to the confusion. We're taking a chance, but I believe it's worth it and will work."

"You're darned right it's worth it!" growled Randal. "I'm itchin' to line sights with those horned toads."

"You'll get the opportunity, all right," Slade answered. "Well, guess we have time for a smoke. It'll be a while yet before they show."

He drew the makin's from his shirt pocket and deftly rolled a cigarette. Randal tried to also roll one, but he was shaking with excitement and spilled the tobacco. Slade smiled and passed him his completed brain tablet and began the manufacture of another.

"Darned if I believe you've got any nerves at all," Randal grunted as he accepted the smoke.

"I'm more used to this sort of thing, that's all," Slade replied, touching a match to his cigarette.

CHAPTER
TEN

They had still quite a while to wait after the butts were pinched out and cast aside. Slade glanced anxiously at the darkening sky; there wouldn't be much more daylight. He strained his ears, caught a sound, still some distance away — the bleat of a tired and disgusted steer.

"Coming," he told Randal. "Get set, but don't start shooting till I tell you. This thing must be handled perfectly or we'll end up with the hot end of the branding iron."

A few more minutes and around the bend bulged the heads of the lead cows. And with them came a billowing cloud of dust that all but obscured the following column of cattle. The riders, bunched in the rear, were but moving shadows. Slade shook his head.

"Hate to do this, but it's the only way," he muttered regretfully. "We've got to throw them off balance." He raised the Winchester, waited until the head of the column was almost opposite and fired two shots so swiftly they blended into one.

Down went two of the lead steers, kicking furiously in their death agonies. Others fell over them, effectually blocking the trail. Instantly there was confusion, utter and compounded. The following cows tried to swerve, and could not because of the encroaching brush. They bucked, wallowed, tried to turn. Those behind tried to surge forward. The riders were caught in the welter. Slade swung the rifle around and fired at the dimly seen shadows as fast as he could pull trigger, the ejecting lever a flashing blur. Randal cut loose with a volley of yells and shot with both hands. Slade's great voice chimed in.

Shouts, curses arose. A scream of agony soared to a wailing whimper. Another chopped off short. Answering slugs cut leaves and twigs, but the back of a maddened, rearing horse is not a good shooting stance and none of the bullets found a mark.

A blast of wind swept the dust cloud away for an instant. Slade saw a tall man looming above his fellows and mounted on a splendid bay horse. It was Veck Sosna, he felt sure. He swung the Winchester muzzle to line with the outlaw leader, but the dust cloud whipped back and again there was nothing to shoot at but shadows. Weaving the muzzle back and forth, he sprayed the width of the trail with lead. Dropping the empty rifle, he whipped out his Colt and emptied that also.

Above the hideous turmoil sounded a voice, clear, bell-toned: "Back! It's a trap! Hightail!"

Slade muttered a curse; he'd know that voice anywhere. Sosna was still unscathed.

There followed a pound of receding hoofbeats dimming swiftly to silence. Slade turned to where Shadow waited, then turned back. To try to ride through that churning pandemonium of slashing horns, splaying hoofs and charging tons of flesh would just be a very unpleasant way to commit suicide.

"Easy, they'll quiet shortly," he told Randal as he reloaded his gun. "Fork your bronc and ride out onto the trail while I keep an eye on things. That will hold them and they'll soon turn and start drifting back to their accustomed feeding grounds. I think we did for a couple of the hellions and very likely they're under the cows and not pretty to look at. We're taking no chances, though. That sort only wounded is dangerous as a broken-back rattler. I'll be ready for any move. Go ahead."

Randal did as directed. The sight of the horseman in front quickly quieted the cows and caused them to turn. Soon they were plodding back up the trail.

Two bodies lay in the dust, torn and trampled and mangled almost beyond human semblance.

"Blazes!" Randal mouthed as he gazed at them. "I feel mighty like being sick."

"Hate to touch them but we've got to find out what's on them," Slade said. "I'll take care of it."

His gorge rising, he set himself to the grisly task and quickly unearthed two of the stiff white masks cut with eyeholes.

"The blankety-blank Faceless Riders!" Randal swore.

"Of course, but I wanted to be sure," Slade replied, dropping the blood-spotted cloths in the dust. "Yes, the Faceless Riders, and the big hellion on the bay is the head of the outfit. Thought I had him, but the dust blew back and saved him. Well, maybe his luck won't hold forever.

"Yes, the Faceless Riders. Still trying to even the score. They knew, or thought they knew, that everybody would be busy building the ranchhouse and figured it would be a good chance to knock off a few thousand dollars' worth of cows. So they slid in through the hills and made a try at it."

"And if it wasn't for you, they'd have gotten away with it," growled Randal. "I keep getting deeper in your debt all the time. Say! I bet they were the fellers Carter, the range boss, saw riding past the other night."

"Very likely," Slade agreed. "They left Marathon ahead of us, leaving one man to handle the dynamiting scheme. Chances are they had the raid in mind all the time. Your deciding to leave yesterday afternoon instead of spending another night in town sort of tangled their twine for them, as it were. Well, we might as well shove those cows back to pasture and head for home. And I think you'd better send word to the sheriff of what happened."

"Don't figure the devils will be holed up somewhere waiting for us?" Randal asked apprehensively.

"Not them," Slade reassured him. "They won't draw rein till they're sure they're in the clear. They're thoroughly demoralized, and they don't know how many were holed up here waiting for them. Besides, it'll be dark in another half hour, which wouldn't be favorable to a drygulching. We've nothing more to worry about today. Later on will be something else again." His black brows drew together as he spoke.

For he had indulged in no mere figure of speech when he employed the plural pronoun. The vindictive Sosna would undoubtedly include George Randal in his feud with *El Halcon*. Which gave the Ranger no little concern. He had grown quite fond of the old rancher and hated the thought of something bad happening to him. Well, it was typical that one problem always gave birth to others.

Shoving the tired cows along was slow work and it was very late when they finally reached the half-completed ranchhouse, to find everybody badly worried.

"Was just figuring to come looking for you," said Jeff Carter, the range boss. "What in blazes kept you out till this time of night?"

Randal told them in detail. Carter swore himself blue in the face. The hands ably seconded his efforts. Felipe ran a thumb along the razor-edge of his biggest butcher knife.

"All right," Carter growled ominously. "If it's war they want, war they'll get."

"They got some today, thanks to Slade," Randal observed cheerfully. "The way they sifted sand! For ten minutes after they were out of sight you could still hear them whiz!"

Felipe had food hot and waiting, and plenty of coffee, of which Slade and Randal partook heartily.

"Now what?" asked the rancher as he pushed back his empty plate.

"Now I figure a little ear pounding is in order," Slade replied. "Tomorrow I plan to ride to Boquillas for a talk

94

with Alvarez. We can lay the groundwork for the construction men who'll arrive early next week. Tomorrow is Friday."

"And I'm riding with you, and so are half a dozen of the boys," Randal stated flatly. "We're taking no chances with those wind spiders from now on."

A wrangler took charge of Randal's horse, but, as was his habit, Slade cared for Shadow himself, giving him a good rubdown after he'd finished eating.

"It's been a long trail but looks like we've finally hit paydirt," he told the black. "That big jigger was Sosna, no doubt in my mind as to that. I got a bare glimpse of him, but it was enough. Looked sort of like he'd grown a short beard since we saw him last, but that didn't change his general appearance. He'd stand out in any crowd, even with one of those white masks over his face. Lance-straight, graceful as a panther, no mistaking him. And hisvoice confirmed it. I don't think I ever heard another voice with that bell-tone quality. Yes, looks like we're nearing the end of the trail, one way or another."

Shadow snorted dubiously, as much as to say that what the end would be was a toss-up. Slade chuckled and headed for bed.

However, he did not go to sleep at once, for he was plagued by an unanswered question: Where the devil did Sosna hole up between raids? In Boquillas, Mexico? Slade didn't think so. A man of his outstanding appearance would attract attention and be remembered, and so far as he'd been able to learn, nobody had noted the outlaw chieftain. He'd investigate that angle more thoroughly when he reached the Rio Grande town.

He was still pondering the problem the following morning when he rode south accompanied by Randal, Jeff Carter, young Harve Yost and four other Walking R hands. Yost's bullet-slashed cheek was healing nicely, but there would be a scar.

"A few more like it and I'll be real purty," he declared.

"A dozen couldn't hurt your looks any," observed Carter. "A feller can be just so ugly and that's all. Yes, a few more might be an improvement."

"Envy's an awful thing," sighed Yost. "Not that you can blame him much, though. With a map like that I reckon he envies even a horned toad."

CHAPTER
ELEVEN

The trip to Boquillas proved uneventful. They forded the river and headed for the Puerto Rico Mine buildings. As they drew near, Slade noted several lean, sinewy, dark-faced men lounging about at strategic points. They eyed the visitors keenly but made no move against them.

"Some of Alvarez' mountain Yaquis," explained Randal. "He's brought 'em in from his big ranch to keep an eye on things. They'll do it, all right. Wouldn't want to have a wring with them. They're a salty bunch. Gives you a sorta funny feeling in the back of the neck when those cold dead eyes look you over."

Slade was willing to agree with Randal's estimate. He'd had some dealings with the grim, silent men of the mountains and knew they were second to none in courage and fighting ability.

Carter and the hands headed for Roberto's *cantina*. Slade and Randal entered the office. A girl seated at a desk turned to greet them. She was a very pretty girl with flashing dark eyes and curly black hair.

"Hello, Iris," Randal said. "You look plumb at home."

"I am," she replied in her soft voice. "Mr. Alvarez is wonderful to me, and so is everybody else here. I don't know how to thank you, Mr. Slade, for what you did for me."

"Rather, I should thank you," the Ranger smiled. "Besides, it was Mr. Alvarez' notion in the first place."

"But he asked your advice in the matter, and followed it," she pointed out.

"That's the way with a woman," chuckled Randal. "Gives all the credit to the feller she wants to. Well, I don't blame her. Oh, to be fifty again! Or even fifty-five or sixty!"

Iris colored prettily. Slade laughed, his eyes dancing.

"Right now he's younger than either of us," he said. "Just pretends to be old to throw folks off balance."

"I think you're right," she agreed. "It's a man's attitude toward life, not his years, that decides whether he is young or old."

Slade regarded her with interest and approval. She was even more charming, he thought, in the simple dress she wore than in the short-skirted, low-cut and spangled dance floor costume. And her manner of expressing herself was not at all that of the average dance floor girl. He wondered what her background was, and made up his mind to try and find out.

Old George noted his glance and his eyes twinkled.

"Al around?" he asked.

"He's below ground right now, inspecting a new drift, but he should be back shortly," Iris replied. Randal's eyes twinkled again.

"I'm going over to Roberto's place and have a drink with the boys," he said with elaborate casualness. "Be seeing you, Slade."

Iris watched him out the door, and her eyes were mirth-filled.

"That was rather obvious, dont you think?" she said.

"Yes, but rather nice, don't *you* think?" Slade countered.

Her color rose again. She shot him a glance through the silken veil of her dark lashes and answered softly, "Yes."

Slade sat down and fished out the makin's. "Mind if I smoke?" he asked.

"Of course not," she consented. "I do myself, now and then. All the floor girls do, especially the *senoritas*, but I have trouble rolling them."

"I'll roll one for you," Slade offered. She shook her head, smiling.

"Not here," she said. "I feel I must be somewhat prim in the office."

"I don't think Alvarez is overly prim," the Ranger said. "He's got a twinkle in his eyes."

"He's fine," Iris said. "First thing, he got my aunt and me a house over here. A much better one than we had across the river. He said he didn't want me making the trip back and forth every day."

"He's right," Slade agreed. "Yes, he's okay."

Iris hesitated. "Would — would you like to have dinner with us tonight, Mr. Slade?" she invited. "My aunt is a wonderful cook."

"I'll be glad to," he accepted heartily. "That is, on a condition."

"A condition?"

"Yes, that you stop 'mistering' me. I think you know my first name."

"All right — Walt," she smiled.

At that moment, the graying, distinguished-looking Alvarez entered. His eyes brightened as they rested on Slade.

"Well, so you made it okay!" he exclaimed, shaking hands warmly. "Any excitement?"

"A little," Slade admitted. "I'll tell you about it later. Work on the conveyor will start Tuesday or Wednesday. Everything taken care of and set to go."

"Fine!" applauded Alvarez. He nodded to Iris.

"She's a find," he said. "I did myself a big favor when I took her on. I detest book work and always have trouble getting somebody who won't get things tangled. She's taken all that off my shoulders. Yes, she's a find. The answer to a tired old mine manager's prayer."

"Maybe you'd better sign *her* to a ten-year contract," Slade suggested.

"That's an idea, all right," Alvarez agreed. "I've been trying to get him to sign one, Iris. What do you say?"

"I think I'd be glad to," the girl replied. "Especially if — if Walt does decide to sign."

Alvarez roared with laughter. "There's an inducement for you, Walt," he chuckled. "You better think on it seriously."

"I will, very seriously," Slade promised.

100

"Did Randal come along with you?" Alvarez asked. Slade nodded.

"He and the boys are over at Roberto's, having a drink."

"We'll join them in one," Alvarez said. "Iris, you can take care of these letters while I'm gone. Come on, Walt."

Slade smiled and nodded to her, and followed Alvarez from the office. Iris' gaze followed him through the door.

"Try and get him to sign anything that'll keep him in one place!" she murmured aloud. "Well, he'll be here for a few weeks, anyhow."

The Walking R hands were making the most of this unexpected celebration in town, and the Boss was doing nothing to dampen their enthusiasm. They greeted Slade and Alvarez vociferously and insisted they have a drink with them.

After the drink, Slade and Randal and the mine manager retired to a quiet table where they could talk. Randal proceeded to regale Alvarez with a graphic account of the happenings at Marathon and elsewhere. Alvarez listened in silence, shaking his head from time to time.

"Looks like you've both got trouble on your hands," he said when the rancher paused.

"And those horned toads may not know it, but they've got trouble on their hands, too," growled Randal. "We'll give 'em trouble till it runs outa their ears!"

"Don't underestimate them," Alvarez warned. "They're bad, and they've proven they're bad."

"Uh-huh, but they aint had much luck since Slade showed up," Randal pointed out. "And between you and me and that whiskey glass, they're liable not to have any luck from now on."

"Maybe not," Alvarez conceded. Slade said nothing. Knowing Veck Sosna as he did, he was not as optimistic as the spread owner.

"Well, being as we're here, I guess we might as well eat," suggested Randal. Nobody objected and he beckoned a waiter. They had finished their meal and were enjoying a smoke over final cups of coffee when a lame man with a cane and wearing glasses limped in, waved a greeting to Alvarez and made his way to the bar. It was Brent Dumas, the crippled ranch owner.

"I'm going over and talk with him," Alvarez said. "About ready for some more beef. That's what my hellions live on, beef and whiskey."

"Ask him to come over and join us," said Randal.

"I'll do that," Alvarez replied. He walked to the bar and conversed with Dumas for some minutes, finally returning to the table alone.

"Said he had to leave right away," he explained. "Just stopped in for a drink before heading back to his ranch. He looked tired. I've a notion he pushes that game leg a mite too hard. I've noticed that's often the way of folks with an affliction; they drive themselves. Trying to prove to themselves that they're just as good as they would be without it."

"Sorta like we old fellers do," chuckled Randal. "Trying to show Father Time that we're still a long jump ahead of him. Don't fool that old jigger, though. He closes the distance mighty fast and before we know it he's breathin' down our necks."

A moment later, Dumas placed his empty glass on the bar and limped out, leaning heavily on his cane, his eyes peering through the thick lenses of his glasses. Slade thought he did look weary, like a man who'd had very little sleep of late.

"Dumas wanted me to ride down to his place tomorrow and look over what he's got to offer," Alvarez continued. "But I told him that now that you are here, Slade, that I planned to have you visit the new drift tomorrow and give me your opinion on its layout. Tomorrow is Sunday and the mine will be closed down, but I'll have a man on the job to operate the winding engines. The Puerto Rico is a shaft mine. Okay?"

"Okay with me," Slade replied. "I'd like to have a look at your holding."

"Fine!" said Alvarez. "Now what?"

"Now, I suppose you have an engineer's transit or a Y-level somewhere around?"

"Haven't got a level, but there's a transit in the tool-room," Alvarez replied. "Need it when we're laying out new drifts."

"That'll be okay, especially if it is equipped with a spirit level on the telescope and magnetic compasses, which I suppose it is if it is used underground."

"Yes, it is," Alvarez said, shooting him a curious look.

"Then this afternoon I'll get busy and lay out the emplacements to expedite the work of the construction men when they arrive. I want to do that myself, for I'm particular as to how those towers are anchored. A trifle out of the perpendicular can mean trouble. Perhaps you can dig up somebody to handle the surveyor's rod."

"I'll handle the rod for you," Alvarez offered. "I've done it before and am familiar with it.'

"That'll be fine," Slade said. "Well, I'm ready to head back to the office and get started, if you are."

"I think I'll hang around with the boys for a while," Randal said. "See you later."

Slade and Alvarez repaired to the mine office, where the transit and the surveyor's rod with its graduated numbers were quickly procured. On the site he had chosen for the conveyor tower, the Ranger took careful sights, measuring distances not with chain or tape but by noting the spaces on the rod Alvarez held as intercepted between the two horizontal spider lines on the reticle, a method of great accuracy when accompanied by expert calculation. He measured horizontal angles and vertical angles, and lined points in a vertical plane which would correspond to the tower from which the cable would be suspended.

They crossed the river in a boat and repeated the procedure on the Texas side. After which they returned to the office, where Slade got busy with pencil and paper, working out equations, drawing diagrams, while Alvarez and Iris watched him in silence.

After a while, he straightened up and riffled the sheets together.

"That should do it," he said. "With this they have all the data required and can start work without delay."

Alvarez shook his head. "You become more of an enigma all the time," he declared. "I'm not an engineer, but I know enough about the principles of engineering to recognize one, a good one, when I see him. Why the devil are you riding the chuck line, anyhow?"

"I was born and brought up on the range," Slade smiled reply. "I guess it's in my blood."

Alvarez grunted, but refrained from further comment. Iris regarded him, still in silence, and her big eyes were very soft.

Alvarez glanced at the clock. "Time to shut up shop," he announced. "Going to eat at Roberto's, Walt?"

"Iris has been so kind as to invite me to dinner at her place," Slade replied.

"Then you're in luck," the manager said. "I ate there the night of the house warming. Mrs. Lake, Iris' aunt, is one fine cook. I'll be seeing you at the *cantina* if you drop in later. Think I'll spend the eveing there. Feel the need of a little relaxation. Place isn't the same with Iris gone, though."

"Oh, one dance floor girl more or less doesn't make much difference," Iris replied airily.

"Depends on the girl, eh, Walt?" Alvarez chuckled.

"It certainly does," Slade agreed, with emphasis that caused Iris to blush. "I'll see you there later, though!"

As they left the office together, he remarked, "Iris Lake! That's it?"

"Yes," she answered. "Aunt Agatha married my father's older brother. They owned a small ranch in Presidio County but lost it during the bad time a few years back."

"Which puts us in something of the same boat," Slade observed. "My father lost his, also. Iris Lake," he repeated. "A very pretty name, and it becomes you. A rainbow over still water."

She glanced at him through her lashes. "Still water runs deep, or so they say," she remarked demurely.

"And a rainbow is noteworthy for the beauty of its curves," he countered. Which caused Iris to blush again.

They walked on, charmed to silence by the beauty of the evening. The sun lay low in the west on a purple cloud and softened the rugged loom of the mountains with its mellow light. Birds sang sleepily. Boquillas hummed cheerfully in anticipation of Saturday night and the morrow, a day of rest. It was a peaceful scene despite the wild wasteland that hemmed in the town on every side. The Rio Grande was a sheet of molten gold, with the lonely grandeur of the Texas Big Bend beyond.

"There it is," Iris suddenly said. "Nice, don't you think? A lot bigger than we really need, but Mr. Alvarez insisted that we take it. He said it was formerly occupied by a foreman of his who moved back to Texas and left all the furnishings behind. Frankly, I think he surreptitiously furnished the place before we moved in; all the furniture appears surprisingly new to have undergone use. He is very generous."

"Yes, he is," Slade replied as they turned into the flower grown yard of the comfortable-looking white house. "But don't forget, he has a weighty reason for being nice to you. It is unlikely that those two drygulchers would have left any witnesses if we'd walked out of the *cantina* together and into their line of fire."

Iris shuddered. "It was terrible," she breathed. "I hate to think of — of what might have happened."

"Well, it didn't, thanks to you, and that's all that counts," Slade said cheerfully.

Aunt Agatha proved to be buxom, bustling and jolly, with beautiful, laughing eyes and a ready smile; she was quite a ways from being old. Slade liked her at once. She greeted him warmly, shaking hands with a man's vigor, and insisted on getting dinner underway at once.

"No, I don't want any help," she told Iris. "You stay here with your company. Goodness knows you haven't talked of anything else since first you met him."

"Aunt Agatha! You're impossible!" Iris gasped, her face the color of a very pretty pink rose.

"Hmmmph!" said Aunt Agatha. "When a woman talks of anything other than a man, she quickly becomes boresome, especially if she is talking to another woman. Get along with you!"

Slade shook with silent laughter. "Iris, you're a very pretty girl, and a charming one, but I've a feeling Aunt Agatha can give you cards and spades and still beat you to the draw," he chuckled.

"She's so terribly frank," Iris sighed.

"And does a lot to bolster a man's ego," he said. "But with the unusual circumstances attending our first meeting, it was not illogical that you should discuss it at length."

"That's a nice way to let me down easy," she answered.

The dinner was really excellent and Slade did it full justice. Aunt Agatha smiled and dimpled as she watched him ply a busy knife and fork.

"That's one of the reasons why I like to have a man around the house," she observed. "A man eats; a woman pecks. Discouraging when you cook for only a woman."

Abruptly she made a suggestion. "Walt," she said, "Iris tells me that you'll be around for at least a few weeks. Why don't you stay here with us? We've plenty of room and you'll eat better than at those *cantinas*. I know Mr. Alvarez will expect you to stay at his place, but he's a bachelor and a bachelor's house usually isn't much of a home. We'll make you comfortable."

"Well, after this dinner it would be hard to say no. I'll take you up on it, if you'll allow me to pay my way."

"Oh, sure," Aunt Agatha replied. "No use arguing with you on that point. I know it wouldn't get me anywhere. Okay, then?"

"Okay, and *gracias*," Slade replied. The soft light was back in Iris' eyes as she smiled approval.

"I'll bring my traps over tomorrow," he added.

"We'll give him the big room at the head of the stairs. The one across the hall from yours, Iris," Aunt

Agatha went on. "I sleep downstairs," she told Slade. "I like to be close to my kitchen."

"I have a feeling right now that a room close to the kitchen would suit me, too," Slade said.

"Oh, I guess you can toddle downstairs if you feel like having a cup of coffee and a snack," Aunt Agatha replied. "You're welcome to do so any time you feel in the notion. We want you to make yourself at home."

"I'm beginning to feel that way already," he declared, with a glance at Iris, who lowered her lashes.

CHAPTER
TWELVE

The dishes had been washed and put away and they were sitting in the living room chatting when there was a knock at the door. Aunt Agatha opened it to admit a handsome, distinguished-looking gentleman who swept the floor with his *sombrero* in greeting.

"I was wondering," said Ramos Alvarez — for it was he — if the ladies wouldn't like to spend an evening at Roberto's *cantina*. It's gay and quite interesting there tonight."

"I sure would," Aunt Agatha instantly accepted. "How about you, Iris?"

"I'd like to see the girls again," Iris replied. "You'll come, wont you, Walt?"

"Was already figuring to drop in there later," Slade said. "I want to see how Randal and the boys are making out."

"Come on, Iris, let's change," said Aunt Agatha. "Be down in a minute, gentlemen."

It was a little more than a minute, but not a great deal, when both reappeared looking, Slade thought, very charming. Alvarez seemed to think so, too, as his eyes rested on Aunt Agatha. Walt Slades face wore a pleased expression as he looped Iris' arm in his and

110

they left the house, leaving Alvarez and Aunt Agatha to follow.

"She's glad of a chance to get out," the girl said. "After all, she's not old; she was only seventeen when she married my uncle, less than twenty years ago. He was a good deal older but they got along fine together."

"I've a notion it would be hard for a man not to get along with her," Slade replied. "And I've a notion that goes for the whole family, judging by what I've seen of it," he added.

"I hope you'll keep on thinking so," Iris said, her color rising a little.

"I will," he stated with finality.

As they left the house, Slade noted that three lean, dark-faced men in *vaquero* clothes sauntered along unobtrusively not far behind. He smiled, for he recognized them as Alvarez' fierce mountain Yaquis. Evidently the mine manager was taking no chances. And he admitted to himself that it was comforting to have those grim fighters as a bodyguard. Their eyes would miss nothing, and if occasion arose, they would swing into action with hairtrigger speed.

The *cantina* was crowded and lively. Roberto instantly spotted them and came forward bowing and smiling to conduct them to a table.

In answer to a nod and a sideways glance from Alvarez, Roberto found another table nearby for the Yaquis, who sat sipping their wine and apparently paying no attention to what went on around them. But Slade well knew that not a man entered the place who didn't get a thorough once-over.

111

"I think I'd like to be a dance floor girl," remarked Aunt Agatha. "It appears to be an interesting life."

"It is," Iris agreed, "only it's darn hard on the feet. The boys don't mean to step all over you, but when they've had a few drinks their aim isn't always so good. They're not all like Walt, who dances divinely."

"That I intend to prove, and right away," Aunt Agatha said with alacrity. "Come along, Walt, be nice to an old lady."

"Truly, I am honored," Slade replied. "And I only wish I could think I am really as young as you."

"Very gallantly said," she replied with a trill of laughter. "Come along."

As they glided out onto the floor, she said, "I've a notion my young niece is very much smitten."

"As to that I'm not so sure, but I think I can name one who really is smitten," Slade answered.

"And what do you mean by that?" she asked.

"I mean I never saw Alvarez so spick and span," Slade replied obliquely.

The beautiful, youthful eyes looked up into his. "You mean he's interested in Iris?" she asked innocently.

"No, I don't mean that, and you know I don't," Slade countered. "And incidentally, I consider Ramos Alvarez one of the finest men I've met. Also, I have a feeling he's a mite lonely."

Aunt Agatha sighed. "I can understand that," she said. "I get lonely myself sometimes. The Bible says it is not good for man to live alone; that goes double for a woman. Oh, well, I guess I've no right to complain; life hasn't been too bad to me. And Iris was right. You do dance divinely. Let's go back to the table and give Iris a chance. I feel the need of a drink."

George Randal, looking somewhat the worse for wear, came over to join them for a moment.

"The boys are still whoopin' it up, but I figure I've had about enough heck-raising for one day," he said. "I think I'll go to bed."

"Okay," said Alvarez. "My major domo will let you in, and you know where your room is. See you tomorrow."

The ranch owner headed for the door, weaving somewhat. He waved his hand and vanished into the night.

"I guess George, like myself, is feeling the years a bit," Alvarez commented. Aunt Agatha glanced at him through her lashes, and smiled.

Slade had several dances with Iris. Meanwhile he studied faces, listened to scraps of conversation, and learned nothing he considered of interest. The evening passed pleasantly and without incident; it was late when they left the *cantina*.

After seeing the ladies home, Slade and Alvarez headed for the latter's house, the silent Yaquis trailing behind. Alvarez walked in silence for some time, then abruptly remarked, "Mrs. Lake is certainly a fine woman. She has a delicious sense of humor."

"And she's very nice looking, charming, and an excellent cook," Slade added, gazing straight to the front.

"Yes, she's all of that," Alvarez agreed. "She told me you are going to board with them while you are here.

113

You're lucky to have the chance for a little home atmosphere. I have a good cook and all my creature comforts are meticulously cared for, but I'll admit that at times the life of a bachelor is — well, a bit dreary. You're still too young to understand that, but you will sometime if you don't stop mavericking around and settle down."

"It's a condition that can always be remedied," Slade said gravely, but with the devils of laughter in his eyes leaping to the front.

"Perhaps," Alvarez conceded. "Perhaps, that is if — well, I guess we'd better go to bed if we hope to get a fairly early start to the mine tomorrow. It's just a short ride to the pit head, but we may be some time below ground."

Despite the fact that he still hadn't the slightest notion as to the whereabouts of Veck Sosna's hangout, or how to drop a loop on the slippery devil, *El Halcon* went to sleep in a fairly complacent frame of mind. Looked like certain things were going to work out in a satisfactory manner. Walt Slade liked to see happiness come to others.

The following day, Slade and Alvarez headed for the mine. Leaving Boquillas they followed a long slope that led gently upward for a mile or more. When they reached the crest, Slade turned in his saddle and gazed back the way they had come. The trail to town lay empty, shimmering in the sunlight. He faced to the front again and rode on.

"I'd originally planned for us to make this inspection trip Monday instead of today," Alvarez suddenly observed. "I'd made arrangements with the workers to have the drift cleared for us tomorrow afternoon; they're blasting and it isn't a good notion to amble in there without giving advance notice. Accidents sometimes happen. But when I talked with Dumas yesterday I changed my mind. I want to look over the stock he has to offer, but Monday will do just as well. I got to thinking it might be a good notion for you to be free tomorrow in case the construction people might show up a day earlier than expected. And the drift will be clear for us today. I'll countermand my former order."

"Not a bad idea," Slade agreed. "The folks from Laredo might make better time than they figured on."

It wasn't a long ride to the mine. Arriving there, they found a young Mexican, not much more than a boy, lounging in the door of the building that housed the winding engine, who greeted them cordially and with respect.

"I will put the *caballos* in the barn," he said. "The cart mules are out on pasture."

"I always bring the mules up Saturday afternoon," Alvarez explained. "I figure they've earned a day above ground in the fresh air.

Slade nodded approval. It was like Ramos Alvarez, he thought, to give consideration to even the animals that worked for him.

The engineman was properly introduced to Shadow and the big black allowed himself to be led to the barn and a helpin' of oats, along with Alvarez' mount.

"The cap lights are ready, also hand lamps," the engineman said when he returned.

"*Gracias*, Juan," replied Alvarez. "We may be below ground for quite a while."

"I'll be waiting for your signal," said Juan. "Go you with God."

"A dependable young fellow," said Alvarez as they took their places in the big cage which hung over the dark and yawning mouth of the shaft. "Been with me nearly ten years, now. I'd trust him with anything. I took him on when he was just a little ragged *muchacho*. Caught him trying to pick my pocket."

"Trying to pick your pocket!"

"Well," said Alvarez, almost apologetically, "he was so little and so ragged, and so hungry looking, with a pinched face and big eyes. There he was, holding his little ragged arm across his face, expecting to be thrashed. But he didn't whine, and his eyes never left mine. So instead of walloping him, I asked him how a plate of roast beef would go!

"'Roast beef!' he exclaimed, awe in his voice. 'I could eat a whole cow roasted!' Been a long time now since he was hungry, I reckon."

Walt Slade gazed down at the mine manager from his great height, and his cold eyes were suddenly warm and sunny.

"'In as much as ye did it unto one of the least of these my brethren ye did it unto Me!'" he quoted softly.

Ramos Alvarez bowed his head, and looked very pleased.

116

CHAPTER
THIRTEEN

At the manager's signal, the cage shot downward. The Puerto Rico was a deep mine and it took some little while to reach the lowest level. Slade and Alvarez stepped out into utter blackness and the silence of the tomb.

Above their heads towered a vast web of interlocking timbers that held the walls of the gutted lode apart. The timbers were massive, and the framework stretched upward beyond the reach of the eye in the closing gloom. Had they a hundred hand lamps, still the summit of the structure would not have been visible. It was like the clean picked skeleton and ribs of some colossal prehistoric monster. A great beam was laid on the floor, then upright ones, usually about five feet high, supporting another horizontal beam, and so on, square above square like the framework of a window.

Slade studied the vast lattice for some minutes while Alvarez watched him.

"Well, what do you think of the construction?" he asked at length.

"Not bad," Slade replied. "Wall plates and end plates are well placed, and so are the stulls, but I'd say the interstices are a bit wide. These are not narrow stopes

117

— excavations where the ore has been removed. Have you had much trouble with rock falls?"

"Very little," Alvarez said. "The walls of base rock on either side of the ore vein are usually pretty solid. Some galleries we haven't had to timber at all."

Slade nodded and did not comment further at the moment. He knew that Mexican mining men, even the best of them, their knowledge and methods inherited from their forebears, the Spaniards who gave little thought to the safety of the Indian slaves they forced to work the mines, were liable to be lax in such methods.

For a long time they trudged through the silence and the dark, pausing from time to time to inspect some gallery by the light of the lamps, which cast small circles of radiance against which the blackness beat like a living thing. It was eerie and even depressing in the vast underground excavations now deserted by the miners. During work days it would be a scene of bustling activity, with lights winking in every direction, but today there was only the utter stillness and the dark.

The shadows crept after them, like predatory beasts crouching to spring. They crowded close on either side, retreated reluctantly before the advancing light, seeming to bide their time, waiting, waiting!

Slade, sensitive to all impressions, experienced a growing presentment of evil, of hidden menace. It appeared ridiculous to think that anything untoward could happen here in the silent, tenantless mine. But the feeling persisted. He caught himself glancing over his shoulder, half expecting to see some monstrous shape materialize from the darkness. He muttered under his breath and resolutely faced to the front. The encroaching blackness and the utter silence were getting him jumpy, that was all. Alvarez certainly didn't appear affected, for he trudged on blithely, pointing out things of interest.

Finally they came to the mouth of the tunnel which was the beginning of the gallery that would be driven downward into the bowels of the earth, following the vein of ore. Here Slade, who missed nothing, commented on an unusual phenomenon: "Quite a draft pulling into this crack."

"Yes," Alvarez explained. "It was mighty stuffy and the air was bad, so a bit farther on we drove a shaft to the upper level to provide ventilation. She's a lot better now."

"A good notion," Slade said. "In a tunnel like this, if you should happen to have a bad rock-fall, men could be suffocated by dynamite and lamp fumes. A good safe-guard against loss of life."

That shaft would prevent loss of life in an unexpected manner.

As they entered the tunnel, Slade held his handlamp aloft and studied the rock roof. It was cracked and seamed and fissured. He shook his head in disapproval.

"That roof should be timbered without delay," he said. "Should have been timbered as you went along."

"I've got the timbers ordered, and the embrasures in the base rock are cut ready to receive the uprights," Alvarez replied. "Farther along it's solid enough."

"Don't delay," Slade advised. "Any subterranean disturbance — and you're near enough the earthquake belt here to experience one — might well bring that roof down. And if it did come down, it would be curtains for anyone who happened to be caught under it."

"I'll get after it right away," Alvarez promised.

Slade did not comment further, but it was another example of the laxity of which he did not approve.

After a while the tunnel curved sharply, and no great distance beyond the bend the rock roof showed improvement, as Alvarez said it would.

They walked on, stumbling at times over chunks of broken stone that littered the floor, passing the shaft to the upper level, which was equipped with a ladder for the convenience of the workmen. Finally they reached the blank face of the tunnel.

"A few more hundred yards and we'll commence driving down through the vein," Alvarez said. "Well, I guess this is it, and we've been underground for quite a while. You approve of what you've seen?"

"Everything is okay except that section of roof near the mouth of the tunnel," Slade said. "A good, clean cutting," he added, examining one of the embrasures that would receive the vertical timbers of the gallery. "These are sunk deep enough and properly faced. But don't neglect that roof shoring job. You're flirting with trouble if you do."

"I'll take care of it right away, and I'll hold up further work on the drift till it's put in shape," Alvarez said.

"Well, I guess we might as well be getting above ground."

They turned and began retracing their steps. They were not far from where the tunnel curved when Slade abruptly halted.

"Hold it!" he said in low tones. "Didn't you say nobody was in the mine today?"

"That's right," Alvarez replied. "Why?"

"Douse your lights," Slade ordered, snuffing out his own before answering the question.

"Because there's somebody in it now, and right in this tunnel. I just caught a whiff of tobacco smoke coming along on the draft."

Alvarez had obeyed Slade's order without question. Now they stood in utter darkness.

"There it is again," Slade whispered. "Somebody not far ahead is smoking a cigarette. Quiet, and listen."

Standing motionless, they strained their ears. "Did you hear it?" Slade breathed. "Somebody stepped on one of those rock fragments and it crunched under his foot. Quick, against the wall, into this embrasure. I don't like the looks of things."

He moved silently into the cutting in the wall as he spoke, gripping Alvarez' arm so as not to lose touch with him in the darkness. And the unpredictable happened.

Alvarez dropped his handlamp. It struck the floor with a clang of metal like to a thunderclap in the great stillness. Ahead sounded a sharp exclamation.

Slade slammed Alvarez against the back wall of the embrasure as the darkness fairly exploded to a bellow

121

of gunfire. Lead stormed past, whining through the air, knocking sparks from the stone. Slade dropped his lamp, jerked his Colts and fired at the flashes.

A yell of pain echoed the reports, another, and a wild scuffling of feet on the loose stones. Then more shots, clipping past the shallow niche, ricocheting with lethal whines. Slade shoved a gun around the rocky edge and fired three quick shots. Answering bullets ducked him back into the niche.

Silence followed, then a couple of more shots, from nearer at hand.

"They're sliding along the wall toward us," he breathed to Alvarez. "Get ready for a showdown. There must be at least half a dozen of the hellions."

"Can't we slip out and make a run for the shaft?" panted Alvarez.

"They'd hear us and sweep the tunnel with lead," Slade replied. "We've got to fight it out right here. Steady, now, I think they're getting ready to rush."

Crouching, listening, he could make out the faint shuffle of slow steps. A pause, while his nerves tensed to the breaking point. He thrust his gun muzzles forward, triggers drawn back, thumbs hooked over the hammers. He could hear Alvarez breathing hoarsely.

Dead silence! Then a thundering volley. Then, as the Ranger tensed to meet the attack, another sound, a crackling and rending; then a thunderous crash that rocked the very mountains. Displaced air howled past, slamming Slade against the rock wall. Dazed, half-deafened, he faintly heard a squealing cry knife through the darkness, like the dying squeal of a squashed rat. It sank to a rattling moan. Then silence, utter and complete.

"Good heavens!" panted Alvarez. "What was it?"

Slade raised a hand to his suddenly damp face. "A little while ago, I was censuring you for not shoring up that roof ahead, but right now I'm darned thankful you didn't," he said in a strained voice. "The vibrations set up by the gunfire loosened the broken rock and the roof came down. And those devils are under it! I feel uncommonly like being sick."

Alvarez gulped in his throat, as if feeling much the same way.

"You all right?" Slade asked anxiously.

"How could I be otherwise with you keeping me behind you all the time?" the manager retorted. "It's a wonder to me that one of those slugs didn't get you."

"One nicked my arm, nothing serious," Slade admitted. "This hole in the rock saved us. That and the fact that one of the hellions carelessly lit a cigarette at the mouth of the tunnel, not counting on the updraft. If I hadn't gotten that whiff of tobacco smoke we would have walked right into them with our lamps going, and would never have known what hit us. At least in this world. That was what they planned on, of course; they expected to see us coming. Now let's light the lamps and give things a once-over."

They lit the cap lights first, and by their aid retrieved and lighted their handlamps. The glow of the flames showed a jumbled mass of splintered stones extending from the tunnel floor to the roof.

"We'll have to go back and climb the shaft ladder to the upper drift," Slade said. "Let's go, I'm worried about Juan."

"Do you think they did for him?" Alvarez asked as they retraced their steps to the shaft.

"I don't know, but they would have had to get him out of the way so they could use the elevator to lower them into the mine," Slade replied. "They must have left one of their number aboveground to raise the cage at signal. He's due for a mite of surprise," he added grimly, his eyes the color of frosted steel as he thought of the pleasant Mexican youth fouly murdered. And he heartily hoped against hope that Veck Sosna was one of the crushed bodies beneath the fallen roof.

He hoped, but not too hopefully. Somehow he couldn't see Sosna caught in such a trap; his luck just didn't run that way. But maybe he remained aboveground to operate the winding engine, leaving the drygulching in the depths of the mine to his followers. That *would* be a break. *El Halcon* caressed the butt of his reloaded Colt.

The climb up the ladder to the next level was arduous but not difficult for active men. Then after a long tramp they reached the shaft and descended to the lower level by way of another ladder.

Slade approached the cage warily, but it was empty, and in answer to his signal it began to rise.

"Keep back," he told Alvarez. When the elevator reached the surface he stepped out, thumbs hooked over his double cartridge belts.

In the engine room door stood a man who stared unbelievingly, gave a yelp of alarm and went for his gun.

Slade drew and fired with both hands, left and right. The outlaw died, the Ranger's two bullets laced through his heart, his hand still gripping the butt of his unleathered gun. Slade raced forward, stepped over the body, and entered the engine room.

Juan lay huddled on the floor, an ugly gash in his scalp just above his left ear. Slade knelt beside him.

"Not dead," he told Alvarez, who came panting through the door. "Just knocked out. I don't think he's badly hurt. Get some water and we'll bathe his wrists and temples and see if we can bring him out of it. There's a cook shanty here, isn't there? Good! Get a fire going as soon as you fetch the water. Some hot coffee will do him a world of good when he comes around.

Alvarez brought the water and hurried to the cook shanty. Slade sponged Juan's wrists and temples and washed the cut, by which time Juan was muttering with returning consciousness. Slade sat back on his heels and rolled a cigarette. A moment later Juan opened his eyes and stared dazedly about. With Slade's assistance he sat up, holding his head in his hands.

"Now suppose you tell me what happened?" Slade suggested.

"*Capitan*, I hardly know," Juan replied. "Seven men rode up to the mine and asked me if they were on the right road to Boquillas. I told them that they were and they asked permission to water their horses at the trough, which of course I granted. Two of them came into the engine room and began asking questions about the machinery. I thought nothing of it, for folk are often curious about the workings of the mine. I turned to point to the indicator gage and was struck from behind, after which I knew nothing."

Slade nodded. Of one thing he was certain: Veck Sosna was not a member of the raiding party. Otherwise, Juan would not have been left alive!

"Sit still and take it easy," he told the Mexican, and left the building. From his saddle pouch he took bandage and ointment, noting that the seven horses tied to one of the racks bore no brands. By the time he had the wound smeared with ointment and bandaged, Alvarez appeared with steaming coffee, of which Juan partook gratefully. Slade helped him to his feet and they walked to the cook shanty, where Slade and Alvarez also drank coffee.

These matters attended to, Slade gave the body of the dead outlaw a careful once-over.

"A native of *Mejico*, with much *indio* blood, I would say," observed Alvarez, gazing at the swarthy face with its high cheek bones and glazed, beady eyes.

"Very likely," Slade agreed. He began turning out the slain man's pockets, revealing nothing of significance other than considerable money which he passed to Juan.

"A little payment for your cracked head," he explained. "No white mask on this one, but just the same I'll wager he was one of the Faceless Riders."

126

"Without a doubt," agreed Alvarez. He began counting on his fingers. "Seven today. One in Marathon, I believe you said. Three who tried to drygulch you and George. Two the other night in Boquillas. Hmmm! That makes thirteen, Walt. I don't think there are many of the devils left."

"But the head of the outfit is still sashaying around and, as I have said before, that sort of a head grows another body mighty fast. However, they may be slowed down a bit for a while, which should help, I hope."

"Oh, yes, and Dumas did for one. That makes it a baker's dozen, and one over," chuckled Alvarez. "At this rate, the head will have to do some mighty fast growing to keep pace."

"Now I reckon we might as well head for town," Slade said. "Come on, Al, and we'll get the rigs off those critters and turn them into the pasture to graze. Then we'll saddle up and ride. Juan, you stay here till we're ready; I think you can make the trip."

"I'm all right, *Capitan*, except for a headache," the Mexican youth replied with a wan smile. "And perhaps as we ride, *El Capitan* will tell me what happened underground."

"Yes, I'll tell you," Slade promised, rising to his feet.

"Wait!" exclaimed Alvarez. "I had forgotten your arm; you were wounded."

"Just a scratch," Slade deprecated the injury. However, at Alvarez' insistence, he bared his left arm to reveal a slight bullet crease which he permitted the manager to treat with the ointment, refusing a bandage.

In the course of the ride to town he regaled Juan with an account of what happened in the mine. The Mexican swore picturesquely in two languages.

"Surely, *El Dios* was with you, *Capitan*," he declared.

"And some mighty fast thinking on his part," added Alvarez. "I wouldn't have noted that tobacco smoke or realized what it meant."

After which Slade did some more thinking, seriously. How the devil, he wondered, did the hellions know he and Alvarez intended to inspect the new drift. Looked like the wrong pair of ears must have been listening to the conversation Alvarez held with Dumas in the *cantina*. Which meant that one or more of Sosna's men had been present. Sosna himself was not there, that was sure for certain; he would have spotted the big sidewinder at once. Well, he had gotten the breaks, and sooner or later the horned toad would slip, he hoped.

Upon reaching town, Juan, feeling much better, was sent to his nearby home. Slade and Alvarez cared for the horses. Slade shouldered his saddle pouches.

"I'm taking them to Mrs. Lake's place," he explained. "Got some clean clothes and my shaving kit and a few other necessaries in them. Come along with me, Al. You'll be the better for a home-cooked meal and a little companionship this evening."

"Do you think I'll be welcome?" Alvarez asked doubtfully.

"I don't think; I know," Slade smiled. "Come along!"

The welcome both received was certainly not lacking in warmth and Alvarez was quickly at his ease.

"Iris, show Walt his room," Aunt Agatha directed as she donned an apron and headed for the kitchen.

Iris did so. "I hope you'll be comfortable," she said softly.

"I'm sure I will be *very* comfortable," Slade replied, glancing at the half-open door across the hall — which revealed a chamber of feminine daintiness — and back to his charming companion.

Under his laughing regard, Iris blushed hotly. But she did not appear displeased, and the glance she slanted him through her lashes was something in the nature of a challenge.

CHAPTER
FOURTEEN

When Slade arrived at the mine office the following morning, he found Alvarez already busily at work.

"I told the boys to clean up that mess and haul out the bodies." he said. "I also ordered them to shore up the roof as they advanced, to take no chances with it."

"Good!" Slade applauded. "That cracked roof served its purpose, and we don't want an encore that could end in a tragedy."

"And now," said Alvarez, his face suddenly grim, "and now we are going to visit the *alcalde* of this town. I desire to have a little talk with that horned toad."

They found the mayor of Boquillas in his office. Alvarez' brow was black as a thundercloud as he faced the official.

"You!" he roared. "What good are you? What good are your so-called law enforcement officers? And the *rurales*, your mounted police, which our good governors placed at your disposal whenever you might feel the need of them — where were they?"

"D-don Ramos!" stuttered the astonished major. "What is amiss? What have I done?"

"What have you done!" stormed Alvarez. "It is not what you have done, but what you have not done! An honest citizen cannot inspect his property without running the risk of being murdered. You allow a hotbed of out-lawry to flourish right under your warty nose! I am writing to His Excellency, the governor, today. I predict that unless a reformation occurs, and quickly, there will be some changes made around here."

"Please, tell me what has happened to so enrage you," begged the thoroughly frightened *alcalde*.

Alvarez told him graphically and profanely. The mayor shook his head and clucked sympathetically.

"Now get busy," Alvarez concluded. "Call out your *rurales*. Set your so-called police force to work, and clean up that nest of snakes or you will hear from me again. In two short weeks, *Senor* Slade here has done more to curb their nefarious activities that all of you put together."

"He is not a law officer," muttered the mayor, glancing askance at the tall Ranger.

"No, praise be to *El Dios*," retorted Alvarez. "If he was, and of the same caliber we have here, doubtless I would be dead. Get busy!"

As they left the office, with the thoroughly perturbed *alcalde* shouting orders to his clerks, Alvarez snorted, "I told him!"

"You certainly did," Slade agreed, shaking with laughter. "But don't be too hard on him. He's just a small-town official who, I fear, is up against something too big for him to handle."

"I'm afraid you're right," Alvarez conceded. "What we need here is some Rangers from Texas — a pity they have no authority here."

"They pack considerable authority on their hips," Slade smilingly replied.

"Yes," agreed Alvarez. "And that's the only kind of authority those scoundrels understand and respect."

Slade smiled again and did not comment father.

An hour later the construction force from Laredo boomed into town a day ahead of schedule and the banks of the Rio Grande became a hive of activity. Big John Cassidy, the construction foreman, studied the data Slade supplied and favored him with a look of respect.

"This will greatly expedite the work," he said. "What company are you with sir?"

"The Puerto Rico Mining Company, at the moment," Slade replied, with a smile. Cassidy turned to Alvarez.

"You are fortunate, sir," he said. "Very fortunate."

"Yes," Alvarez agreed dryly. "In more ways than one."

George Randal showed up around noon, chipper and cheerful.

"Been quite a weekend," he chuckled. "Now I'm heading for the spread to see how my new *casa* is coming along. But I'll be back soon, me and some of the boys. What you fellers been doing? You'd done vanished away when I got up yesterday morning. Didn't show up at all last night, did you?"

"I'm staying at Mrs. Lake's place," Slade explained. Alvarez deftly changed the subject.

"We had quite a day of it yesterday," he said and proceeded to graphically describe the day's happenings. Randal swore pungently when he paused.

132

"Looks like they're after you hot and heavy, eh?" he remarked to Slade.

"Yes," the Ranger replied. "So much so that I still think it would be a good notion for you two to fight shy of me for a while."

"We've been through all that before," Randal replied.

"And we're not going through it again," Alvarez added. "We're in this fight together, all three of us, till the last brand is run. Now I'm going out again and watch my conveyor system take shape. Be seeing you, George."

"And soon," said Randal as he headed for the stable and his horse.

"I sent word to Dumas to shove along whatever stock he thinks best," Alvarez remarked to Slade. "I haven't time to ride down there today. I can trust him to send me good stuff. Right now I'm too interested in what's going on here to leave."

It took the Puerto Rico miners four days to clear the rock-fall and retrieve the bodies of the six drygulchers. Slade, Alvarez, the *alcalde*, and George Randal, who had returned to town, rode to the mine to view them before they were carted away for burial.

They were not a pretty sight, the human body not being constructed to resist the impact of tons of rock dropped from a height.

"Recall seeing any of them before?" Slade asked the *alcade*. The mayor shook his head.

"Even if I had, I doubt if I would recognize them now," he said. "You believe they were members of the *ladrones* called the Faceless Riders?" Slade nodded.

"Well, they're 'faceless' now, all right," said Randal. "Blazes, what a mess! I've seen all I want to see."

"Take them away," Alvarez ordered.

Slade did not go through the dead men's pockets. He knew perfectly well that the Puerto Rico miners had already attended to that chore, doubtless to the profit of the local *cantinas*.

"Of one thing I am sure," the mayor said thoughtfully as the mangled remains were borne away. "None were natives of *Mejico*, although the one *Senor* Slade shot, the one nobody could recall ever seeing before, undoubtedly was."

"Which is interesting," Slade remarked. The mayor glanced at him questioningly, but the Ranger did not see fit to amplify the remark.

"My *rurales* are searching the hills for those who may remain alive," the mayor said.

"Here's hoping they have luck," Slade replied. Frankly, he did not think they would; Veck Sosna was too crafty for the Mexican mounted police, even were his hole-up somewhere in the hills south of the Rio Grande, which Slade did not believe was so.

Meanwhile, work on the conveyor system was progressing. The towers, solidly foundationed, were rising. At first Cassidy, the construction foreman, had questioned the excavation depth Slade insisted on.

"You don't know 'Ol' Debbil River'," Slade told him. "It has a nice little habit of changing its bed every now and then. Where you're standing right now may be under three feet of water next week. I want those foundations secure against possible undermining by the current."

Cassidy scratched his head and agreed that Slade was right.

With the transit, Slade took frequent sights and carefully calculated just what degree of cable slant, south to north, would be productive of the best results and insure proper gravitational travel by the loaded ore buckets and the least power required to draw the empties back to the south shore.

"He's an engineer, all right, and a good one," Cassidy confided to Alvarez. "A nice feller, but don't get him riled. The other day big Tim Roberts, who's a tough *hombre*, started to question one of his orders. Mr. Slade just turned those smoky eyes on him and Tim shut up in a hurry. Yes, he's a nice feller. When he smiles at you he makes you feel good all over, but I wouldn't want him to look at me without smiling and mean it. Funny thing in a *cantina* the other night. I heard some cowboys talking. One of 'em said he is an outlaw."

"Then so is Padre Miguel of the San Vicente Mission," snorted Alvarez.

Cassidy chuckled and nodded assent.

Meanwhile, Walt Slade was doing some hard thinking. More familiar with the workings of the outlaw mind than most, he felt that Sosna's followers might quite likely be in a state bordering on panic. Things hadn't been going at all well with them of late. Which meant

135

trouble for Sosna. An outlaw leader cannot stand still, content to bask in the aura of past accomplishments.

Right now it was urgent that Sosna do something that would bolster the courage of his followers, what was left of them, as well as enable him to acquire suitable recruits to replace losses and build up his dwindling force. Some daring and lucrative exploit was absolutely necessary. Knowing Sosna as he did, *El Halcon* did not doubt that without delay he would attempt something of the sort. He told himself morosely that he would have to step lively or whatever nefarious scheme the outlaw had in mind might well be crowned with success.

And the devil of it was, he hadn't the slightest notion as to where and when Sosna might strike.

CHAPTER
FIFTEEN

A salt cart driven by a tattered Mexican rolled into Boquillas, Texas. It forded the river, its high wheels churning the shallow waters of the Rio Grande, which was very low at the moment. After threading the narrow streets of the mining town it pulled up before a side door of the Puerto Rico Mine offices. The salt was shovelled into containers and taken away, while the driver in ragged clothes puffed leisurely on a husk cigarette and watched proceedings with eyes that were singularly keen and alert for one of his calling. A close observer might have noted that he wore two guns under his closely drawn *serape*. He peered back into the body of the cart and nodded to a couple of the mine guards who loitered nearby. These at once came forward.

For the driver was removing the floor boards of a false bottom to reveal, snugged beneath, a number of stout and plumped-out canvas sacks, which appeared to be very heavy for their size. These were carried into the office and carefully stowed in the big iron safe.

"Ingots from the mills," Ramos Alvarez said to Slade. "We employ all kinds of dodges to fool gentlemen with share-the-wealth notions. This is one of them. Salt carts ply back and forth all the time between the salt flats to

137

the north and Mexico; would take an army to keep an eye on all of them. We've never yet lost a shipment via salt cart."

"Sounds like a clever method," Slade conceded. Alvarez nodded to the safe.

"A lot of dinero represented by those pokes," he said. "Our silver ore has a very large gold content, more so even than the Comstock Lode in Nevada. Tomorrow it will be transported south, under a heavy *rurale* guard — we sell to the Government."

At about the same time as the arrival of the salt cart, the small herd of beef cows from Brent Dumas' Square D ranch showed up. Dumas did not ride with the herd; it was brought in by three of his riders, lean taciturn men who did their work with speed and efficiency. The cows were quickly weighed and corralled. Alvarez paid for them with money taken from the safe and counted across the desk to Dumas' range boss, who was one of the three who handled the drive. The range boss signed a receipt and departed.

"Never has much to say, but he knows his business and is dependable," Alvarez commented. "Dumas has a good bunch riding for him — brought them here with him when he took over the ranch."

"All Texans?" Slade asked.

"So I would presume," Alvarez replied. "At least they are all Americans, of that I am sure. Yes, a good bunch though rather clannish. They don't mix much and stay together when they're in the *cantinas*. Not unusual, though. After all, they are in what they doubtless consider a strange land, and I don't think any of them speak Spanish."

"Most Texans know a little," Slade commented. "Not all, of course, especially those away from the Border country."

"That's so," Alvarez agreed. "I don't think Dumas speaks any. I think he is from northeast Texas. You speak it like a native. I think some folks are born linguists, though, and you're an example. Well, I guess we'd better be calling it a day. The night watchman is already here and wondering why we don't leave so he can go to sleep in comfort. Iris, at this rate I'll have to start paying you overtime."

"You're paying me enough as it is," the girl replied. "Besides, I like conversational overtime. Are you coming home with Walt and me for dinner?"

"Not this evening," Alvarez declined. "I want to have a talk with *Senor* Gomez, the bank cashier, at Roberto's. I may drop in later."

"Speaking for myself, *and* Aunt Agatha, you'll be welcome," Iris answered, her eyes laughing. Alvarez tried to look dignified, and failed signally.

After a bountiful and excellently prepared dinner, Slade and Iris sat in the living room and talked. Mrs. Lake was busy in the kitchen, baking a cake.

"Mr. Alvarez is very fond of chocolate layer cake," Iris had whispered to the Ranger.

Slade was restless. Once again he was beset by a presentiment of evil, a disturbing premonition that something untoward was about to happen. What it could be he hadn't the slightest notion. But the feeling persisted, and he had learned not to disregard such hunches, as he called them. It was in fact just another manifestation of the peculiar and unexplainable sixth sense that develops in men who ride much alone with danger as a constant stirrup companion. Abruptly he suggested, "Iris, what do you say we drop over to Roberto's place for a while?"

"I'm for it," the girl replied. "I think," she added with a giggle, "that Aunt Agatha will be glad to get rid of us for a while. I told her Mr. Alvarez might drop in later, and you'll notice she's wearing a new dress under that apron. I'll tell her we're going."

Roberto's *cantina* was busy and lively. They found a table near the dance floor and sat down.

"There's Mr. Alvarez now, talking with Mr. Dumas, the rancher, and *Senor* Gomez, the bank cashier," Iris said.

Slade nodded. He had already spotted the trio at the bar. Alvarez turned and waved to them, then continued his conversation with Dumas and Gomez, an elderly man with a dark but pleasant face. Shortly he turned again and sauntered to the table, Gomez following. Dumas, however, did not accompany them but limped out, leaning heavily on his cane and, as usual, peering uncertainly through his glasses.

"Just wanted you and *Senor* Gomez to know each other," Alvarez said. "We were discussing the shipment of the silver ingots tomorrow."

Slade shook hands with Gomez, who declined the offer of a drink, explaining that he had a business engagement.

"Iris and I figure to stick around a while," Slade told Alvarez, who said good night and left the *cantina* with Gomez.

"And once he's outside he'll leave Gomez," Iris giggled. "Yes, it was a good idea you had, and I think we should stay here quite a while."

"Are you envious?" he asked.

"Do you think I have any reason to be?" she retorted. "Anyhow, I'll have you for a while," she added, a trifle wistfully. "It will be a nice memory."

"Memories have a habit of becoming realities, sometimes," he said.

"Yes — sometimes. Let's dance."

They stayed at the *cantina* until nearly midnight and walked home slowly under the stars.

At the door Slade paused. The "hunch" had abruptly assumed definite shape.

"You go to bed," he told the girl, "I'm going to walk around a bit."

She gave him a searching look. "Are you going to get into trouble again?" she asked.

"I certainly don't look for trouble," he replied.

"I'm not so sure," she said. "Sometimes I think you do."

Slade kissed her lightly. "Don't worry about me, I'll be all right," he said.

"I hope so," she said as she closed the door, very softly, and did not look convinced.

Slade walked slowly to the corner, then quickened his pace. He headed for the mine office by a circuitous route that avoided the busier streets. He approached the side of the building in which the door that led to the small inner office was located. As he drew near he saw that a low light burned in the outer office. Which in itself was not strange; the night watchman might keep it going for his convenience. But somehow that lurid glow had an ominous look.

The Ranger studied it intently for several minutes, from a patch of shadow. Then, carefully keeping in the shadow, he circled to the rear of the building and, hugging the wall, crept cautiously toward the side door. Suddenly he stumbled and nearly fell. His forward questing foot had touched something yielding. For a moment he froze against the wall.

There was neither sound nor movement from the thing. He bent down, peering, and just made out the dim form of a human body. His exploring hand touched a face that was cold, rigid of feature. He straightened up, tense, alert. At his feet lay a dead man, and there was little doubt in his mind as to who it was.

The night was very still, with only the muted murmur of the town below the office site to break the silence. Then abruptly he heard an alien sound, which he recognized as the petulant stamp of a horse not far off. And he knew no horses had been left outside the barn!

For moments he stood gazing in the direction of the sound, which was not repeated. He could see nothing in the gloom. Then he stepped over the body of the murdered watchman and resumed his stealthy approach to the door. As he neared, a dim gleam from a street light showed that it stood ajar.

Beside the narrow crack he paused, peering, listening. Gradually he became conscious of yet another sound. A rat gnawing in the wall could have made such a faint but persistent sound, only there was a thin rasp to it as if the rat were gnawing metal, which no respectable rat would try to do. The sound seemed to come from the outer office. He reached out a careful hand and pressed against the door. It moved back noiselessly on oiled hinges. When the crack was large enough to admit his body, he eased through the opening into the back office.

For another moment he paused, flattening against the wall, then glided forward until he could peer through the door of the outer office.

He saw the forms of three men. One was squatting before the big office safe, deftly manipulating a drill, the bit of which was eating into the iron near the combination knob. He was a broad-shouldered man, evidently tall; that was about all Slade could make out in the dim light. His companions leaned forward watching the progress of the drill.

Slade dropped both hands to his gun butts and opened his lips to speak. Then he whirled at the sound of a step behind him. Outlined against the beam of the street light, a man loomed in the doorway. Slade caught a gleam of shifted metal, drew and shot with both hands even as the other pulled trigger. He reeled against the wall as the slug burned a red streak along his neck, and the gun fired again.

A gasping cry echoed the report. A choking and gurgling and a thrashing about of arms and legs as the man went down. From the outer office volleyed startled exclamations. Slade spun about, caught a glimpse of a towering form and blazing black eyes as a hand swept the lamp to the floor and darkness blanketed the room. Instantly he hurled himself down. Lead stormed over his prostrate form. He fired at the orange flashes, again and again. There was a crash of a door flung wide open. He leaped to his feet and dashed forward, tripped over something and fell headlong.

The impact was so severe that for a moment he was stunned and floundered aimlessly. By the time he was able to lurch to his feet, he heard a patter of fast hoofs outside the building, swiftly fading away. With an exasperated oath, he holstered his guns and fumbled a match from his pocket.

"And I'll wager a hatful of pesos that *he* got in the clear as usual," he growled to the unresponsive dark as he struck the match.

The flicker of the tiny flame showed what he had fallen over. It was the body of a man with a blue hole between his eyes. It also showed the drill lying on the floor, the bit still stuck in the door of the safe.

The match winked out. Slade struck another, procured a lamp from the inner office and touched the flame to the wick. The man lying by the door was a bloody mess, the slug having struck him in the throat. Slade scowled at the huddled form.

"Not your fault, but my own stupidity," he told the dead man. "If I'd used my head for something other than to hold up my hat, I'd have realized the light from that street lamp would outline me against the door as I slipped in. And I should have remembered that very likely somebody would be left outside to hold the horses and keep a watch on things. If you hadn't kicked the door sill as you came in, and if you'd been just a mite faster with your gunhand, it would be me, not you, lying there."

Feeling better for having castigated himself verbally, he placed the lamp on the floor and turned out the dead man's pockets, revealing nothing of significance save one of the tell-tale white masks and considerable money, which he replaced. A similar search performed on the corpse in the main office was of no better results. Evidently the raiders had so little feared interruption after killing the watchman that they hadn't bothered to don their masks.

Which was characteristic of the crafty Sosna. Doubtless he had thoroughly studied the lay of the land and knew that nobody ever approached the office in the night time. But how the devil did he learn the precious ingots would be in the safe this particular night! Well, he always appeared to be able to learn things that were supposed to be secret.

Slade wondered if the shooting had been heard in town and decided that very likely it had not. All the firing had been inside the building, which was situated some distance from the main streets. Going outside, he examined the body of the watchman and discovered a knife plunged between his shoulder blades. A typical Sosna touch. Trailed while making his routine rounds and struck down from behind.

Returning to the office, Slade considered the situation. It was still not very late and he believed there was a chance that Alvarez might still be visiting with Mrs. Lake. Anyhow, he'd try the Lake establishment first. He wrapped his neckerchief over the bullet burn that had trickled a few drops of blood and set out in search of the mine manager.

Luck was with him in this particular instance. Alvarez, Iris and Mrs. Lake were having coffee and cake in the living room when he entered. Iris gave him a searching look.

"Always wear your neckerchief around your ears?" she asked. Slade threw out his hands despairingly.

"What's the use to try and fool a woman," he said in resigned tones. "See, it's nothing but a scratch."

Alvarez peered close. "Uh-huh," he said, "the sort of scratch a bullet makes when it comes too close for comfort. Guess you might as well tell us what happened. We're all interested."

Holding back nothing, Slade told them. Iris shuddered. Mrs. Lake's beautiful eyes were dark with apprehension.

"Why did you go there alone?" she demanded. "You should have taken somebody with you when, as you admit, you were expecting trouble."

"Didn't have time to hunt up anybody," the Ranger replied. None of his hearers appeared satisfied with the explanation. Alvarez rose to his feet.

"Guess I'd better go over there," he said. "And you say the watchman was done for? Poor old Manuel! He was with me for years. You coming along, Walt?"

146

"Naturally," Slade replied. "So long, everybody, we'll be seeing you. Yes, Iris, I'll be back before long."

"I'll be waiting for you," the girl replied. "And please try and be careful."

"Nothing more to worry about tonight," he said lightly. "Come on, Al."

They departed, leaving two worried women behind.

"You know where the *alcalde* lives, of course?" Slade asked. "Okay, we'd better rouse him up and take him with us. This thing sort of comes within his province, as it were."

"A lot he'll be able to do about it," Alvarez growled disgustedly. "But I suppose he'd better be notified. And you did for two of the devils?"

"Yes, but the big he-wolf of the pack escaped as usual," the Ranger answered gloomily. "Sometimes I'm almost inclined to believe he really does bear a charmed life, as folks have said of him."

Alvarez shot him a curious glance but asked no questions.

The *alcalde* had gone to bed, but he got up again and sent a servant flying to summon his chief of police while he dressed hurriedly. By the time he had gotten into his clothes, the police officer arrived and the four of them made their way to the mine office.

All was as Slade had left it shortly before. He pointed to the drill bit still sticking in the safe door. Five overlapping holes had been drilled.

"Another half hour and the combination knob would have been lifted out and the safe opened," he said.

The mayor shook his white head. "I don't know what we would do without you, *Senor* Slade," he declared. "You appear to be the only person living who can make headway against those *ladrones*. Two dead! Ha! I wish it were more. Poor Manuel! To him we will give decent burial, with mass said for his soul. But this carrion" — he glared at the bodies on the floor — "'twere better to cast into the river and let them go hellward unshriven and unannealed!"

"And poison the fish," grunted Alvarez. "Incidentally, I am offering a reward of five thousand pesos for the arrest and conviction of Manuel's murderers. Post notices, Tomas, and spread the word around. It might induce someone to talk. Don't you think so, Walt?"

"Possibly," the Ranger conceded. Privately he did not think it would, for the simple reason that, in his opinion, nobody other than Sosna's followers knew anything to "talk" about. Veck Sosna took few into his confidence, and those few were bound to him by the chains of fear.

"Well, I guess there's nothing more we can do here," Alvarez said. "Might as well call it a night; be morning before we know it."

The police chief promised to send one of his men to keep watch the remainder of the night, and everybody headed for bed.

"I'll wager Iris is sitting up waiting for you," Alvarez said to Slade. "If she is, tell her not to come in tomorrow until noon. She'll need some rest, and besides I want things cleaned up a bit before she comes

148

in. Not a pretty sight for a girl's eyes, the office right now."

Alvarez would have won his bet, for Iris was sitting up, waiting, when Slade entered the house.

"I couldn't sleep, didn't even try," she answered his disapproval. "How could I? For all I knew, you were right in the middle of something again. You're enough to drive a woman loco, as Mr. Randal would say."

"Wonderful!" Slade chuckled. "How's Aunt Agatha?"

Iris glanced through her lashes and a dimple showed roguishly at the corner of her red mouth.

"She's fine, and sound asleep, or at least she says she is."

"Perfect!" he said, with another chuckle. They ascended the stairs together.

CHAPTER
SIXTEEN

The office had been cleaned up when Slade arrived there the following morning and only the holes in the safe door bore witness to the night's tumultuous happenings. He was in a thoughtful mood as he greeted Alvarez.

"Al," he asked, "who knew the silver would be in the safe last night?"

"Why, the driver and the two guards who helped carry in the sacks. But they're absolutely trustworthy, on that I'd wager my life," Alvarez replied. "Then of course, Gomez, the bank cashier knew. And, come to think of it, Brent Dumas was present when I told Gomez it was ready for shipment."

"Nobody else?"

Alvarez shook his head. "Nobody that I know of, but it seems somebody else did know."

"Yes, somebody else," Slade agreed, still thoughtful, then changed the subject. For he did not wish to discuss with Alvarez, at the moment, the subject of his thoughts.

In fact, he was thinking of Brent Dumas, the crippled rancher, and of the somewhat interesting coincidence that every time something cut loose, Dumas had been in evidence shortly before. Dumas had known of the contemplated inspection trip to the mine. Dumas had known that he, Slade, planned to ride to Marathon. And Dumas had been in Roberto's *cantina* shortly before the attempted drygulching that, had it not been for Iris, would quite likely have been successful.

Of course coincidence could very well be the explanation; plenty of other people had been present each time. Dumas stood out because of his crippled condition and because he was associated with Alvarez. There was certainly nothing apparent to indicate wrongdoing on the part of Dumas.

But there was another angle to consider. Veck Sosna had a genius for making indirect contacts through which he was able to obtain information not put out for public consumption. One of his men might have wormed his way into the rancher's confidence and become quite friendly with him and in the course of apparently innocent discussions learned what Sosna wished to know.

Certainly, aside from the silver, there had been nothing secret about the transactions involved. Indeed there had been little secrecy where the silver was concerned once it passed safely through the wild Big Bend country and arrived in Boquillas. Alvarez had given it so little thought that he did not bother to set special guards to keep a watch on it, although he undoubtedly would next time.

Summing up, Slade resolved to learn what he could relative to Brent Dumas' associates. Just possible that he might uncover the lead he so badly needed.

Several peaceful days followed, with the conveyor system nearing completion. Slade estimated that less than a week would see it in operation.

And then George Randal rode into town and contacted Slade. "Come on over to Roberto's and have a drink with me," he requested. Slade accepted the invitation and they made their way to the *cantina*. It was early afternoon and the place was quiet. Randal chose a table in a corner farthest from the bar. After they were seated and a waiter had taken their order, Randal leaned close and lowered his voice.

"Walt," he said, "I've got something to tell you. I believe those hellions are planning to raid my holding. You remember young Pedro Gonzales, my Mexican hand, the one who tagged you right off as *El Halcon*?"

"Yes, I remember him," Slade replied. "A nice young fellow."

Randal nodded. "Well, Pete is part Comanche and there isn't much he doesn't see. He told me that three times in the past few days he spotted a jigger riding up in the south hills and trying to keep under cover. He was pretty sure the horned toad was looking things over careful. Good water on the south pasture and the grass is better than average. A lot of the cows stray down that way and sort of bunch, especially at night. Wouldn't be much of a trick to round up a few hundred and shove 'em into the hills and on to Mexico, for somebody who knows the trails, and those sidewinders 'pear to know all of 'em.

152

"I've a notion that Pete has the right of it and they are up to something, so I figured that with your help we might be able to set a trap for the snakes and maybe clean out the whole nest. What do you think? I'm just about sure for certain that they are planning something."

"Very likely you're right," Slade returned thoughtfully. "Knowing his methods as I do, I'm pretty sure that Sosna has included you and Alvarez in his vendetta against me."

"Sosna?" Randal repeated, looking puzzled.

Slade abruptly arrived at a decision. "Finish your drink and let's head back to the office," he said. "There's something you and Alvarez should know."

Randal looked even more puzzled, but he asked no questions and tossed off his glass.

When they reached the office, Slade closed the door and turned the key in the lock.

"I don't want any interruptions," he explained. "What I have to say is in strict confidence."

"Then perhaps I'd better leave the place to you, gentlemen," Iris suggested.

"You stay right where you are," Slade told her. "You also have a right to know."

He slipped something from a cunningly concealed secret pocket in his broad leather belt as he spoke and laid it on the desk. The others stared at the famous silver star set on a silver circle, the feared and honored badge of the Texas Rangers.

"Well, I'll be darned!" sputtered Randal. "So that's what you are!"

"Should have known it," said Alvarez. "He does things like only a Texas Ranger can do them."

Iris said nothing, but her eyes were wide, and dark with something akin to pain as she gazed at the gleaming star.

"Yes, I'm a Ranger," Slade said. "Undercover man for McNelty's company. Now I'll tell you the story of Veck Sosna, which will explain why I'm here."

In detail he related his experiences with Sosna in the Canadian Valley country of the Panhandle, and his pursuit of the former Comanchero leader over half of Texas.

"And here I finally caught up with him," he concluded. "He's the most dangerous, most vicious, and cruelest outlaw Texas ever spawned, and she's turned out some prime specimens. He's a genius at attracting and organizing others of a similar nature, and he has what owlhoots usually don't have — brains. And he uses them. He is a charlatan in a way, with a flair for the bizarre — those grotesque hooded masks are an example — but he's deadly. Yes, he's the leader of the Faceless Riders, and so long as he's running around loose you'll be plagued by the Faceless Riders."

Randal and Alvarez exclaimed with profanity as forceful as the presence of a lady would permit. Iris still said nothing, but continued to gaze at the star of the Rangers as if fascinated by its silvery gleam.

"He's utterly ruthless and utterly vindictive," Slade continued. "That's why he has included you two for special attention."

154

"I'll special attention him if I manage to line sights with the sidewinder," Randal vowed. Alvarez suddenly chuckled and produced an envelope from the desk drawer, and drew forth an official looking document which he unfolded ostentatiously and passed to Slade.

"Sort of anticlimax, under the circumstances, but I've been in touch with the Governor of Coahuil and there's your commission as a *rurale* of Mexico," he said. "I thought it might come in handy."

"It very well might, and thanks," Slade said, pocketing the paper. "Especially as Sosna is operating on both sides of the Border and as a Ranger I have no official authority thought it might come in handy."

"I think you pack enough authority with you at all times to get you by on either side of the River," Alvarez commented dryly. "But a commission as a *rurale* removes all danger of international complications which might be posed by some gentleman still waving the bloody shirt of past conflict."

Slade nodded agreement. "And now that things are clarified, late tonight, George, we'll slide across the river and ride to your place," he said. "Perhaps we will be able to set a trap for the slippery devil. The affair will have to be handled carefully, however, for he is daring and cunning and thinks with hairtrigger speed. One little slip-up and we're liable to find ourselves on the receiving end of something we won't like.

"I'll be back to check the completed conveyor system and put my okay on it," he told Alvarez. "Everything is going along nicely. Cassidy knows his business and has followed instructions to the letter."

"Get this other business over with and never mind the conveyor system," Alvarez said. "All of a sudden it is of secondary importance."

Randal was gazing at the safe door. "What happened to the box, Al?" he asked. "It's all full of holes."

Alvarez told him. Randal shook his head and swore under his breath.

"No limit to what the hellions will try," he snorted, glowering at the riddled safe door. His gaze grew contemplative.

"Wonder why the hellion didn't work the combination like he did with mine?" he asked.

"That is a large and very heavy safe," Slade replied. "Not easy to hear the click of the falling tumblers through that thick door. I'd say he figured the drill would be faster and certain. Especially as he evidently thought he would be free from interruption once the watchman was out of the way."

It was well past midnight when Slade said good-bye to Iris and repaired to the stable where Shadow waited expectantly; the big black seemed to know that he was due to get a chance to stretch his legs after a period of tiresome inactivity.

Together with Randal and the three cowhands who had accompanied the rancher to town, Slade forded the river and rode north at a fast pace. They met with no incident and the false dawn had not yet fled ghostlike across the sky when the new Walking R ranchhouse loomed before them.

"And she's a lot better than the old one," Randal observed complacently. "Those carpenter fellers sure know their business. I handed 'em enough of a bonus to keep 'em drunk for a week. Well, we'll have a snack and then knock off a little shut-eye."

When he arose, shortly after noon, Slade questioned Pedro Gonzales about the prowler he spotted.

"Three times did I see him," said Pedro. "Far up in the hills he rode, slowly, looking down."

"Did he appear to be keeping under cover?" Slade asked.

"*Si*," replied Pedro. "But he was awkward. He brushed against the chaparral and it waved. That first I saw. Then I saw the shadow upon which the sunlight rested."

Slade nodded his understanding. The Comanches were the best trackers in Texas and, as Randal said, Pedro had Comanche blood. Quite likely the average person would not have noticed that tell-tale swaying of the growth and the moving shadow behind it. But it was enough to attract the attention of Gonzales, whose eyes were the eyes of a hawk.

After considering all the angles with meticulous care, Slade laid his plans in accordance with the conclusions he reached. Shortly after dark he led his troop due north, turning east in the shadow of the hills and, pursuing the course for halfway to the head of the valley, turned due south.

"I think that if they really mean to try something, they'll strike between midnight and dawn," he told his companions. "It is logical to believe that they have a hole-up somewhere in the hills to the south. There they'll lay over during the daylight hours, planning to reach the Rio Grande after dark."

Slade was in an exultant mood, for it looked like the final showdown with Sosna and his hellions might well be at hand. And with a dozen rifles ready for action, there was scant chance that any of the raiders would escape.

The "posse" continued at a good pace, but it was a long ride and the night was well advanced when the southern hills loomed no great distance away. Slade slowed the gait, studying the terrain as best he could by the wan glow of the stars. Soon they spotted clumps of cows still grazing or standing bunched on the banks of a little stream that entered a narrow canyon. He slowed the pace still more and after a bit uttered an exclamation of satisfaction.

Directly ahead was a grove of trees that formed a solid block of shadow.

"Made to order for us," he said. "We'll hole up there and wait. Nobody can see us, but we can see anyone who rides from the south. Tether the horses and take it easy. Nothing to do now but wait."

It proved to be a long wait. The tedious hours shuffled past on leaden feet. The great clock in the sky wheeled westward, degree by slow degree, and nothing happened. There was the smell of dawn in the air when Slade disgustedly gave the order to return to the ranchhouse.

"Not tonight," he said. "No sense in hanging around here any longer. Let's go."

158

The following night was a wearisome repetition of the one first. The prairie lay silent and deserted save for the grazing or sleeping cattle. And Walt Slade began to grow acutely uneasy. He had an unpleasant premonition that in some manner he had been outsmarted. He wondered if while they were guarding the south, the raiders had struck farther to the north, and, fearing no interruption, had comfortably rounded up a herd and skalleyhooted with it. Could be. At any rate, he didn't feel at all right about the lack of developments.

He was due to feel even worse before long.

When Slade and Randal entered the ranchhouse, they found a visitor awaiting their arrival. Ensconced in an arm chair, his pipe going and a cup of steaming coffee at his elbow, Sheriff Cain Dobson looked the essence of well-being. A glance at his face, however, told Slade that things were not well.

After greeting the Ranger, Dobson cocked an inquiring eye at Randal.

"Go ahead and talk," Slade told him. "George has the lowdown on me."

"Okay," said the sheriff. "I'd expected to find you in Boquillas, but luckily I decided to stop off here for a snack. Well, here goes!"

The sheriff was a good narrator and as the devilish sequence unfolded, Slade felt as if he was an eye-witness to the affair.

CHAPTER
SEVENTEEN

The stage from Alpine to Presidio rolled along blithely. It was a huge, clumsy vehicle drawn by six mettlesome horses, its sides lined with boiler plate. There were no passengers this trip but inside the locked doors were two armed guards. A third, alert and vigilant, shared the high driver's seat with old Hank Brodie, the driver.

The stage carried more than thirty thousand dollars in gold and bills consigned to the Presidio Bank.

The coach passed through Shafter, the trail skirting the foothills of the Chinati Mountains to drop over the cap rock, the heights sliding away in a rubble of debris to the edge of a stark desert where the sun beat down with a scorching, dazzling heat, reflected blindingly from the gleaming sands, where there was no vegetation other than cactus, sage, and the ghostly, snakelike arms of the octillo.

But before reaching the desert, the track wound through a stand of thick growth to cross a creek by way of a wooden bridge. The creek was swollen by recent rains, but the bridge was supported by heavy timbers resting on solidly anchored piers, and the high water posed no real threat at any time.

160

The stage rolled onto the bridge. It had reached the center of the span when there was a sharp crack, a rending and splintering. Down went the bridge, and down went the stage, rolling over on its side in four feet of water. The terrified horses regained their footing, snapped the traces, scrambled up the steep bank and fled.

Old Hank Brodie and the outside guard were flung free to land in the water with a resounding splash. They had barely gotten erect when from the growth bulged five masked men, shooting as they came.

The outside guard fell and sank, a swirl of bloody froth in his wake. Brodie also fell. The current caught his flaccid form and hurled it downstream with astonishing speed. The outlaws poured bullets through the coach window. From inside came screams of pain, then choking moans, and silence.

The raiders slid down the bank and surged into the water. A heavy hammer smashed the lock and the door was dragged open. One scrambled inside and came up dripping, but with the strongbox in his hands. It was a heavy load, all he could manage, but one of his companions, tall, broad-shouldered, with black eyes flashing through the holes in his hooded mask, seized the box as if it were a feather and carried it up the bank.

The hammer was again brought into play. The metal box was knocked open and the gold and bills transferred to the saddle pouches of horses led from the growth. Then the outlaws mounted, forded the stream and thundered south on the Presidio trail.

Old Hank Brodie wasn't dead. A bullet had grazed his forehead and dazed him for a moment. Half-drowned, he managed to claw his way up the bank and into a clump of growth, where he lay gasping and retching and heard the outlaws race past. Regaining his strength somewhat, he staggered upstream to the scene of the outrage. The horses, entangled in the harness, hadn't run far. Brodie had no difficulty approaching them. He freed them of the harness, mounted one and with a makeshift bridle rode at top speed for Shafter five miles to the north, from where the news of the robbery and murder was relayed to the sheriff of the county, who notified Sheriff Dobson of Brewster County against the chance the outlaws might turn that way.

"Yes, it happened out of my bailiwick," the sheriff concluded, "but I thought you ought to know about it."

Slade's face was set in granite lines, his eyes the color of stormy water under a wintery sky.

"Yes, I should know about it, about how beautifully I was outsmarted," he said bitterly. "While I thought I was setting a trap for them, they were setting one for me. And I swallowed the bait, hook, line, and sinker!"

"Wh-what the devil do you mean?" sputtered Randal.

"Don't you see it?" Slade answered wearily. "They planned to get me out of the way, against the chance that I might be managing to keep tab on their movements. That hellion Pedro saw up in the hills wasn't trying to keep under cover, although he made it look that way while making sure that Pedro saw him. So Pedro and the rest of us jumped to the conclusion that they contemplated a little chore of widelooping Walking R cows and reacted accordingly. A typical Sosna trick, and I fell for it, that's all. Beautifully outsmarted!"

"Well, so were the rest of us," growled Randal. "We all fell for it. And no wonder. It was a darned smart trick."

"Yes, but I should have known better," Slade said. "I should have remembered that anything *obvious* where Veck Sosna and his activities are concerned would be something to fight shy of. He thrives on the unexpected, the improbable, the impossible."

"Seems to me I've heard something about the same said of *El Halcon*," Sheriff Dobson retorted mildly.

Slade's tense features relaxed in a smile.

"Well," he said, "this running rukus between Veck Sosna and myself is beginning to take on something of the nature of two empty paper bags belaboring each other." Both his hearers chuckled.

"Wonder how they managed to make the bridge fall?" said Randal.

"Simple," Slade replied. "Sawed the supporting timber nearly through, leaving just enough wood to support the bridge, but not the additional weight of the stage. I recall a somewhat similar incident."

"And he had four hellions with him," the sheriff observed thoughtfully. "He used to ride with a dozen and more. Yes, you're thinning them out, all right."

"Yes, but Sosna himself is still plenty thick," Slade answered morosely. "With nearly forty thousand dollars to divide with his devils, they're solid behind him again till the last brand's run. And he won't have any trouble getting recruits if he wants them. Oh, he took this trick, all right, no doubt as to that."

"Yep, he may have won the battle, but I'll wager my last peso he loses the war," declared Sheriff Dobson.

"Hope you're right, Cain," Slade smiled. "At least it's nice that you still have confidence in me."

"And I never expect to lose it," said the sheriff. Randal nodded emphatic agreement.

"Oh, heck, let's eat," he said. "All this palavering makes me hungry. Then a little shut-eye for all of us is in order. I reckon you were up all night, too, Cain. Wonder where the hellions are headed for?"

"They could turn in any direction before reaching Presidio," the sheriff replied. "What do you think, Walt?"

"I've a hunch it is somewhere in the neighborhood of Boquillas," Slade said. "I'm of the opinion that their hole-up isn't far from there. Anyhow, I'm heading back to Boquillas as soon as I grab off a little sleep."

"But not by yourself," Randal stated with finality. "I'm riding with you and so are some of the boys. From what you've been telling me of that Sosna devil, I wouldn't put it past him to figure you will be riding for Boquillas and act accordingly. We're taking no chances with you."

Slade thought the ride would hardly be hazardous, but he didn't argue the point; Randal could be right. Also, he fell in with the rancher's humor when he insisted that they wait until well after dark before

164

setting out, against the possible chance of some hellion keeping tabs on the ranchhouse.

So it was nearly eight o'clock in the morning when Slade entered the mine office to find Alvarez already at work.

"Nothing bad happen?" he asked, as he shook hands warmly.

"Nothing bad happened at the Walking R," Slade replied. "How's Iris?"

"She's fine. She'll be in shortly," the manager replied.

"And how is Mrs. Lake?"

"She isn't," Alvarez answered.

"Isn't?"

"That's right, she isn't."

"Isn't what?"

"Isn't Mrs. Lake."

"Will you please tell me what the devil you're talking about?" demanded the exasperated Ranger.

"Just what I said, she isn't Mrs. Lake any more. She is now *Senora* Agatha Alvarez."

"Well, I'll be hanged!" Slade exclaimed. "Congratulations, you lucky old horned toad! And my compliments to the bride."

At that moment Iris came in, flushed and radiant-eyed. "I saw you through the window!" she said to Slade. He cupped her slender waist in his hands, lifted her from the floor and kissed her.

"Congratulations!" he chuckled. "Congratulations on acquiring such a wonderful uncle!"

Alvarez sighed. "I'm afraid that in tieing onto a beautiful niece I'm losing the best office girl I ever had," he said. "The niece of an Alvarez can hardly be expected to work in an office."

Iris turned on him. "Listen, my dear uncle," she said. "This niece of an Alvarez is going to keep right on working so long as her work is satisfactory. I like my work and I don't intend to give it up. The day of the emancipation of women is at hand. They are no longer economically dependent on the male animal."

Alvarez grinned sheepishly at Slade. "What am I going to do about it?" he asked.

"You're going to learn fast," the Ranger smiled reply. "For a long time you've had everything your own way. Now you're going to find out what it means to take orders and like 'em."

"I fear you are right," conceded Alvarez. "This morning I was forced to change my shirt, and I'd only worn it a week. And she refuses to move into the big casa. Says the kitchen is too far from the living room. Says she doesn't want to get that far away from me."

He spoke mournfully, but there was a light in his fine eyes that belied the tone of his voice.

Slade's own eyes were suddenly all kindness. How wonderful, he thought, that two lonely people, with the evening of life approaching, should find companionship.

Alvarez seemed to read his thoughts, for he said softly, "And you are responsible. My major domo was right when he said, 'El Halcon! Truly, patron, as was

166

said of Our Lord in the days of old, he goes about doing good!'"

CHAPTER
EIGHTEEN

The conveyor system was finished. Complete from its solidly foundationed towers to its shining cable. A symbol! Linking two great countries in friendship and understanding.

Some such thought drifted through Walt Slade's mind. After the years of turmoil and strife and bitterness, God's purpose was made plain. For here stood Slade the Texan and Alvarez the Mexican in all good fellowship, working together for the common weal.

Alvarez dumped the first shovelful of ore into one of the ponderous buckets. The winding engine snorted, the bucket rose, the pawls clicked and sent it careening across the stream, to where a huge ore wagon waited to receive its contents.

"Come on!" said Alvarez. "Everybody to Roberto's! This calls for a celebration."

The celebration lasted for hours and was unanimously voted a success.

"Two of the finest men I ever worked for," declared Cassidy, the construction foreman, nodding to where Slade and Alvarez stood conversing with George

Randal. "Yes, sir! Gentlemen of the Ould Sod, both of them."

"You Irish claim everything," grumbled big Tim Roberts, tipping his glass.

"And why not?" retorted Cassidy. "Didn't we start everything in the beginning? Sure and the Garden of Eden was in Ireland."

"And Adam was the first Irishman, eh?"

"Of course he was," replied Cassidy.

"Hmmm!" said Roberts. "Seems I rec'lect he was kicked out on his ear."

"That was before Saint Patrick chased the snakes from Ireland," countered Cassidy. "After the snakes were gone, Adam came back and got things moving."

"You can't win," sighed Roberts. "Here's to the snakes!"

Yes, the conveyor system was completed and in operation, and Slade was very well pleased with its functioning. But with the progress of his other chore, he was not at all pleased. Sosna had put one over on him, irritatingly, and the cunning devil still proved as elusive as a wraith. Aside from the one fleeting glimpse in the mine office, Slade didn't seen hide or hair of him. Where the devil did he hang out? Did he ever show his face in Boquillas? Apparently not. Nobody the Ranger had questioned could recall seeing anyone that answered to his description. Still, Slade was convinced that he holed up somewhere in the immediate neighborhood.

That night, before going to bed, he sat long in thought, reviewing every detail connected with his contacts with the Faceless Riders, beginning with the attempted drygulching on the Boquillas trail, when he had taken the white masks from the persons of the slain outlaws. Crossing the room, he drew one of the masks from his saddle pouch and spread it on the bed. Acting on impulse, he slipped it over his head and stood before the dresser mirror.

The darn thing did give the impression of facelessness. Instead of features, only a flat white expanse, in which showed what appeared at a quick glance, to be eyeless sockets. The stiff cloth came below his chin in front and down to the back of his neck in the rear. With an imprecation of disgust, he removed the grotesque thing and tossed it back into the pouch.

But he couldn't toss it out of his mind. He had a feeling that some peculiar significance was attached to it, just what he could not imagine, but the feeling persisted.

A review of the attempt on his life in Marathon was barren of results. There hadn't been enough left of the would-be assassin to examine. The abortive drygulching across the street from the *cantina* had provided no clue to Sosna's whereabouts. The same had to be said of the similar attempt in the depths of the Puerto Rico Mine. Again nothing to tie up the attempt with Sosna. Only in the mine office had there been conclusive corroboration of his belief that Sosna was the leader of the Faceless Riders and operating in the section.

Which was all very well so far as it went, but it didn't go far enough. Sosna was still running loose, and active. With a shrug of his broad shoulders he dismissed the whole aggravating business for the time being and gazed expectantly at the door, which stood ajar.

When Slade entered Roberto's *cantina* the following evening, he saw Alvarez, Randal and Brent Dumas talking together at the far end of the bar. Alvarez called to him to join them, but as he paused for a moment to speak with John Cassidy, who was spending another night in Boquillas, Dumas suddenly glanced at the clock over the bar, said a word to Alvarez and limped out hurriedly, his golden hair and beard gleaming in the lamp light.

"Brent had to leave," Alvarez remarked when Slade sauntered to the bar. "He remembered an appointment and was already late. You haven't met him, have you?"

"No," Slade replied. "He always seems busy or on the point of leaving."

"You should," said Alvarez. "He takes an interest in you since you've been downing the Faceless Riders. As I told you before, until you showed up, he was the only person hereabouts who managed to do for one of the devils."

"Al, do you know who his associates are?" Slade asked casually.

Alvarez shook his head. "Hasn't got any, so far as I know," he answered. "Guess I come as near being one as any. He's civil enough, talks with anybody who speaks to him, but never tries to make friends or acquaintances. Comes in with some of his hands now and then, but they don't mix much either. He 'pears to prefer to go it alone. I've a notion he's a mite sensitive about being crippled and not seeing too well."

"Could be," Slade conceded.

"How many hands does Dumas have riding for him?" he asked.

"He has five now, I believe," Alvarez replied. "He had eight, but he told me three decided a couple of weeks ago to return to Texas. He hopes they'll send along some replacements, for he's short-handed."

"He doesn't hire Mexicans?"

Alvarez shook his head. "Never has. He brought his Texans with him when he came here. Reckon he's had no reason to, so far. Perhaps he will now, if the men who left don't send anybody to take their place. Suppose he'll wait a while, though, before hiring anybody here."

Slade nodded thoughtfully. It would appear that the notion that Dumas might have unwittingly divulged information to one of Sosna's men who had gained his confidence was out. It also appeared that he was getting exactly nowhere. Every lead sooner or later fizzled out. Well, maybe the luck would change sometime. No indications of it so far, though. There was no easy way to catch up with Veck Sosna. As to that he suffered no illusions. If there were to be any breaks, he'd have to make them. Well, he'd made them before and would again, he hoped.

That night he again retrieved the grotesque mask from the saddle pouch, spread it across his knees and glowered at it. All day long the blasted thing had haunted him. Haunted him in a jeering, smugly complacent manner, throwing off vague hints that in its stiff folds lay the solution of the problem which confronted him, mocking his futile efforts to grasp its significance.

He slipped the thing over his head, stood up and again gazed at the reflection in the mirror. It reminded him of something. What the devil was it? Ha! he had it! It was very similar to the mask worn by a headsman of the Middle Ages when he chopped off the heads of those unfortunates who had incurred royal displeasure.

Nobody ever knew who the headsman was. His identity was the closest of closely guarded secrets. He might be the king himself. So in addition to his disguising black garments he wore the mask that not only covered his features but his hair and his beard, if he had one, as well. The only difference between this and the headsman's mask was the color, the headsman's mask having been black. This, snugly fitting, also came well below the chin and completely covered the hair as well.

Suddenly Slade's eyes glowed through the eyeholes. He felt of the back of his head to make sure. Yes, it covered his hair completely.

Covered his hair completely!

For a long moment he gazed at the reflection. Then he stripped off the mask, sat down on the edge of the bed and stared straight in front of him for more moments. With fingers that shook just a trifle, not with nervousness but with eagerness, he rolled and lighted a cigarette, and spoke aloud to the glowing tip.

"The nerve of that sidewinder!"

173

Dyed yellow his black hair. Grew a short beard. Walked like a cripple, and did a darn good job of it. Wore thick-lensed glasses, the lenses very probably just plain window glass, to tone down his flashing black eyes. Walked with a stoop to minimize his height. Peered and hesitated as if far-sighted. Shot one of his men in the back for some reason or other — or, typically Sosna, for no reason at all. Brought in the body and one of the masks, causing everybody to believe he had downed one of the Faceless Riders. Which he had, but not in the manner people thought. And got away with what nobody but Sosna would have the gall to attempt.

For there was no doubt in Slade's mind but that *Brent Dumas was Veck Sosna!*

When on one of his forays, he wore the mask that hid not only his features but his hair and beard as well. After which he doffed it and mingled casually with the citizens of Boquillas and its surroundings, picking up information that enabled him to stage another raid with accuracy and success.

Other incidentals crowded forward to bolster his belief. Dumas always avoided close contact with *El Halcon*, doubtless fearing that Slade's hawk's eyes would penetrate his disguise. And he was always in evidence shortly before something cut loose. Also, something that Slade had long noted was typical of an outlaw when he adopted an alias: almost always it was something reminiscent of his own name. Sosna was part French. So he took a French name, although he

174

did not give it the French pronunciation. A small thing, but another thread in the pattern.

Yes, he now knew exactly where to find Veck Sosna. Fine! But what was he going to do about it? He had not one iota of proof that Brent Dumas had committed an unlawful act on Mexican soil. Should he confront him and accuse him of being Sosna, the Texas outlaw, Dumas would in all probability deny the charge and, conditions and circumstances being what they were, would very likely make his denial stick. In Mexico he was regarded as a respectable rancher and the burden of proof would be on Slade to show that he wasn't. And how was he to back up his contention when he could not point to a single deviation from rectitude on Dumas' part? Charge him with masquerading as a cripple? It was conceded by those who knew, that Veck Sosna had enough lead in his body to make a pig, to say nothing of knife scars and other mementos of conflict. He could well exhibit evidence that he was a cripple, or ought to be. Dyed his hair? No law against that so far as Slade had heard. Besides, it was a well-known fact that Mexicans, especially those of a feminine persuasion, admired blond hair. Which could be regarded as a legitimate means of courting favor with the natives of his adopted country. A trifle silly, perhaps, but not criminal. And as for the glasses he wore, it would take an expert to determine whether or not Dumas' sight was faulty, and Slade didn't have an expert handy.

And any such move as outlined would mean revealing his Ranger connections, which he did not wish to do except as a last resort in a time of dire necessity.

Besides, another angle that must be given consideration, Mexicans were touchy where international incidents were concerned. He might well kick up a row that would have repercussions all the way to Washington.

No, orthodox methods were out. He must either get Sosna dead to rights in Mexico, or somehow lure him onto Texas soil. Either of which promised to be a considerable chore.

He almost felt that he would be justified in denouncing the hellion and shooting it out with him. Almost, but not quite. He was a law enforcement officer and must conduct himself accordingly. Besides, a corpse and cartridge session was always a risky business. Flying lead plays no favorites and innocent people might well suffer.

Anyhow, at the expense of a lot of painful thought and deduction, he had accomplished something. He had changed Veck Sosna from an elusive wraith to a very solid actuality. An advantage in knowing where to make his throw, even though he hadn't the slightest notion how to drop his loop.

After pondering all angles of the situation, he resolved to keep what he had learned to himself as a precautionary measure. So long as he did not know he was suspect, Sosna would, Slade reasoned, keep up his masquerade as Brent Dumas and perhaps grow careless and make a slip.

Slade was confident that Sosna did not know him to be a Ranger and in consequence, thinking that he had only to deal with *El Halcon*, an outlaw with a reputation for horning in on good things other people had started, would take chances he otherwise would not risk. Which was an advantage.

Just the same he was in a furious temper. At times his anger would sweep over him like a gust of wind and he could not think coherently. Anger directed more at himself than at Sosna, although that slippery individual was the recipient of his share as, Slade vowed to himself, he would realize before the last brand was run. *El Halcon* did not take kindly to being outsmarted, and he felt that he had been outsmarted. He could vision Sosna chuckling inside himself as he stood calmly at the bar in Roberto's with *El Halcon* seated only a short distance away and never suspecting that his quarry was almost within arm's reach. The wily devil could experience no more exquisite pleasure than thus putting it over on the man he considered his Nemesis.

Well, the last laugh was the best laugh, as Veck Sosna would realize before all was said and done. Comforted by the thought, he went to sleep in a fairly equable frame of mind.

CHAPTER
NINETEEN

The following day, Slade had reason for being glad he had insisted that the conveyor towers be foundationed on bedrock. The Rio Grande was rising and soon the water would very likely be washing their bases. But the raised approaches he had caused to be built amply guarded against any interruption of the loading and unloading of the ore. Let her rise!

Alvarez was highly pleased with the success of the project and said so, emphatically.

"I sure wish you could stay here with me," he said. "I'm dickering for another mining property and nothing would please me better than for you to take charge of it."

"I'll keep it in mind against the time when I may decide to sever connections with the Rangers," Slade promised. Iris glanced at him wistfully, as one who hopes against hope.

Later, Slade and Alvarez stood and gazed at the swollen river chafing against its banks and swelling over them in places.

"Well," said the latter, "if anybody wants to cross today they'll have to climb into one of the ore buckets."

"Or go across by way of the cable, hand over hand," Slade observed.

"I wouldn't want to try it," said Alvarez.

"Would be quite a chore, but I've a notion it could be done, by a man with strong arms and hands," Slade commented.

"Uh-huh, and one slip and down you'd go," grunted Alvarez. "And nobody could hope to live through Boquillas Canyon with the river this high. I'd prefer the ore bucket. Would be a bit bouncy, but drier."

"I guess it'll be best to stay on this side for the time being," Slade smiled. "Let's go eat. Randal is waiting for us. He's stuck in town till the water subsides.

"By the way," he asked casually when they were seated at a table with Randal in Roberto's *cantina*, "just where is Brent Dumas' ranchhouse located?"

"Follow Carmen Street till it runs into the southwest trail and keep on going," Alvarez replied. "Second *casa* you come to, a big old one set back from the trail but in plain view. Figure to drop in on him?"

"I may, now that I've got a little time to spare," Slade replied noncommittally.

"A good notion," said Alvarez. "He'll be glad to see you."

Slade thought otherwise, but refrained from saying so.

As a matter of fact, Slade did plan to visit the Square D spread, but in an unorthodox manner. By so doing he hoped to possibly get a line on whatever hellishness Sosna planned next. At least he might confirm his belief that Dumas was indeed the notorious outlaw. For although he was convinced that such was the case, there was always the chance that he might be mistaken. He had arrived at his conclusion by way of painstaking deduction; he did not *know* that Dumas and Sosna were one and the same. The last vestige of doubt must be removed. Should he be wrong, by concentrating on Brent Dumas, he could be following a cold trail.

"But in my opinion it's a darn hot one," he told himself. "Anyhow, we'll try and make sure."

It was late when Slade rode along Carmen Street. Most of Boquillas' hard-working populace was in bed. The visiting cowhands and a few diehards were holed up in the *cantinas*. The streets were practically deserted. So was the gray ribbon of trail shimmering wanly into the southwest under an overcast sky through which seeped filtered moonlight.

El Halcon rode warily. It wouldn't do to take chances on this lonely trail. It was fraught with too many unpleasant possibilities. But the track wound on steadily southwest despite its twists and turns, deserted for as far as the eye could reach.

It passed a ranchhouse built in Spanish style, with all its windows dark. Slade rode on.

The second *casa*, Alvarez said. Two more miles and there it was, set in the edge of a grove, looming blackly against the cloudy sky. A window fronting the trail was lighted.

His eyes fixed on the building, Slade slowed Shadow to a walk. He earnestly desired to get a look in that open lighted window, but did not deem it advisable to approach it from the trail. He halted his mount and surveyed the terrain. Back of the house the ground sloped gently upward, scantily brush-grown, to a rounded crest. He believed that from that crest he could get a view of all that went on below.

Turning Shadow from the trail, he rode west, then circled to the south until he was almost opposite the ranchhouse, and nodded with satisfaction. The house and the yard were clearly outlined in the dim light. For a moment he sat studying the approach to the building and resolved on a plan of action. Dismounting, he dropped the split reins to the ground and, cautioning Shadow to keep quiet, glided down the slope, taking advantage of every bit of cover, passing swiftly across patches of moonglow.

It was a ticklish business and hard on the nerves. Continually his vivid imagination pictured a rifle barrel thrust through one of the dark window openings, following his progress, a finger slowly tightening on the trigger. A gush of orange flame and a report he would not hear. It was with a deep breath of relief that he reached the corner of the building without anything happening.

At the corner he paused for a long moment, peering and listening, then rounded it and sidled along the wall, hugging the shadow, setting his foot down each time with the greatest care lest it come to rest on a rolling stone or a dry branch. Almost opposite the window was a single tall tree which cast a grateful shadow. Moving diagonally away from the wall, he slipped into the shadow. A few more paces and he could see into the room and hear voices.

Lounging about, smoking and talking, were five men in rangeland clothes. Hard-looking, alert men whose eyes seemed never still. And — Slade's pulses quickened — striding back and forth, big head bent as in thought, was Brent Dumas. He had laid aside his glasses and his cane and his step was lithe and springy. His heart beating exultantly, the Ranger realized that his hunch had been a straight one: Brent Dumas *was* Veck Sosna!

With ears open, Slade listened to the snatches of conversation that drifted through the window, but learned nothing of significance. It was just the ordinary talk men indulge in and had no bearing on the activities of the Faceless Riders.

Sosna paused. Slade shrank back tensely as his piercing eyes turned toward the window. However, they passed the open square of darkness and centered on his men, who ceased their talk and looked expectant.

"So everything is understood, everybody knows just what to do?" he asked. There was a nodding of heads.

"Okay, then," said Sosna. "This one more good haul and we pull out before that big devil catches on. One little slip on somebody's part and he will."

Again the others nodded. "Things sure haven't been breaking right since he showed up here," one ventured. "And every time we've made a play for him, we've ended up holding the hot end of the branding iron. He's the limit!"

"He is!" Sosna agreed. "The things he did up in the Panhandle were unbelievable. He noses out things nobody else would ever guess, and there appears to be nothing he doesn't see. Right now I feel as if those blasted ice eyes of his were looking at me." He turned toward the window as he spoke.

Walt Slade went away from there. Odds of six to one were a mite on the heavy side. Besides, if Sosna realized he was being spied on he might pull out at once, and then the wearisome chase would have to be resumed. Making all the speed he dared, Slade returned to his horse and swung into the saddle. Even as he did so, he thought he heard a door open and close. Taking no chances, he rode due west for several miles before circling back to the trail and did not draw rein until he reached Boquillas.

Well, one angle was satisfactorily taken care of: Dumas was Sosna, all right. His suspicion had been amply substantiated. But the other and pressing angle remained obtuse, and he didn't mean to throw a pun. What the devil did Sosna have in mind? He wracked his brains for the answer, and didn't find it. Something daring and original without a doubt. And something that promised a big haul. His chore was to prevent it, if possible. But how was he to prevent it if he didn't know what it was? He could only wait and watch. Thoroughly tired out from mental and physical exertion, he went to bed and slept soundly until past noon.

Senora Alvarez, cheerful and bustling, had his breakfast ready for him.

"Poor Iris was badly worried because you stayed out till such an ungodly hour," she said as she sat with him while he ate.

"How'd she know I was so late getting in?" Slade smiled.

"Oh, I suppose she stayed awake until she heard you show up," the *senora* replied airily.

CHAPTER
TWENTY

All afternoon Slade pondered the problem and came up with no solution. Of one thing he felt sure. Whatever was pulled would be on the Mexican side of the river; there was no crossing the Rio Grande via horseback in its present condition.

Several hours after dark he repaired to Roberto's *cantina* for a bite to eat and found Alvarez and George Randal seated at a table.

"Old Rio Grande has got me where the hair is short," Randal said. "Don't know when I'll get home. Oh well, I figure I need a rest."

For some time they sat drinking coffee, smoking and talking. Slade's mind was busy in a fruitless endeavor to fathom Sosna's expected deviltry. He glanced up absently as Roberto paused at the table, a sealed envelope in his hand.

"For you, Don Ramos," the owner announced. "An *hombre* left it and requested that it be delivered to you. Who? I do not know. He handed it to a swamper and departed."

Alvarez took the envelope, tore it open and spread out the single sheet it contained. As he read, his eyes widened with horror and his face whitened. Wordless,

185

with a shaking hand, he passed the missive to Slade, who read:

If you wish to see her alive, bring fifty thousand dollars to the straight stretch of the southwest trail eight miles south of Boquillas. Ride alone, for you will be watched, and at any hint of treachery she will die. You have two days in which to raise the money.

The letter, written in a hand as clear and precise as the wording, was unsigned.

"Who — who do they mean, the *senora?*" Alvarez asked through stiff lips.

Slade's voice was quiet when he replied, but his face was set like granite, and his eyes were terrible.

"No, he means Iris, and he means exactly what he says. But I think we may be able to tangle *Senor* Sosna's twine for him. I know where he'll take her, and I'm pretty sure he *won't* know that I know it. First we'll go to the house and make sure everything is okay there. I'm of the opinion that they tricked her away from the house somehow, but we must make sure."

"Walt," Alvarez said, his voice quivering, "I'd rather pay the money than take a chance that she might be hurt. I can raise it."

Slade laughed mirthlessly. "And do you think he'd release her and leave you alive after the money was paid over? No, you would lose not only your money but your life as well, and she would be carried off into the Mexican mountains, where she'd bring a good price.

Sosna has dealt in women before and knows how to dispose of them. So if you're willing to take a chance — and it'll mean taking a chance, don't doubt that — we may be able to save her."

"I'll take the chance, any kind of a chance," Alvarez replied, his voice abruptly steady again, his black eyes flaming.

"And I said a while back that I wanted to be in at the finish of this blankety-blank Faceless Riders business," Randal broke in. "Let's go!"

"Easy now," Slade cautioned. "Walk out casually. I don't think anybody's keeping tabs on us, but we're taking no chances."

They strolled out, talking together. Not until they were some little distance from the *cantina* did Slade quicken the pace. At the corner, he halted and gazed back the way they had come. There was nobody in sight.

Despite his reassuring words to Alvarez, Slade approached the house with a feeling of dread. He believed Iris had been tricked outside on some pretext or other. But knowing Sosna as he did, he couldn't be sure. One more killing would have meant nothing to the sadistic devil. He sighed with relief when *Senora* Alvarez herself opened the door.

"Iris?" he asked. "Is she here?"

"Why, no," the *senora* replied. "I thought she was with you. A man came with a note, about an hour ago, from Ramos, asking her to come to the office at once. Is something wrong?"

"Let me see the note," Slade requested, ignoring the question for the moment.

She procured it and Slade spread it at the table and beckoned Alvarez. The mine manager scanned it briefly.

"Looks enough like my writing and my signature to be mine," he said.

"Yes," Slade said. "He has seen your signature often enough to copy it with the preciseness that characterizes everything he does."

Alvarez looked utterly bewildered, but Slade did not explain at once. He turned to *Senora* Alvarez and briefly reviewed what had happened.

Some of the carmine left her lips and her eyes seemed to darken to violet. But she was of pioneer stock and when she spoke her voice was steady as Slade's own.

"You will bring her back, Walt," she stated simply, rather than asking. And the Ranger answered just as simply, "Yes, I will."

"But where the devil are we going?" asked Randal.

"To Brent Dumas' ranchhouse," Slade replied.

"What!" his astounded listeners exclaimed together.

"Yes, Brent Dumas is Veck Sosna," Slade said. "I'll explain while we ride. Let's go!"

Senora Alvarez clung to her husband a moment, but bravely waved them good-bye from the door.

"I know that stretch of straight trail to the south," Alvarez muttered as they hurried to the stable. "Rises on both sides, from which you can see the whole stretch in both directions."

188

"And they would be watching to see if somebody was tailing you," Slade said. "See what the set-up would be? Somebody would ride out from the brush. You would hand over the money — and die. Well, we'll see if we can't hand the sidewinders a mite of a surprise they don't expect."

Briefly, Slade outlined his case against Dumas. His hearers swore in wholehearted amazement. "Now I can see how that hellion used to ask indirect questions," said Alvarez. "He'd worm information out of you and you'd never realize it."

"Yes, he's smooth," Slade said as they rode swiftly along Carmen Street. "I consider it largely bull luck that I finally caught onto him."

"I've got another name for it," Alvarez commented dryly. "I'd say it was an outstanding example of smart deduction. Well, the Rangers are noted for such things. Just how do you propose to handle the business, Walt?"

"After we pass the first *casa*, we'll cut west by south," Slade said. "We'll circle around and approach Dumas' ranchhouse from the rear. The odds will be two to one against us, but I figured that if we took anybody else with us the chance of surprising the devils would be lessened, and surprise is vitally necessary. If Sosna was forewarned and realized he had no chance to escape, I wouldn't put it past him to kill Iris out of pure hellishness; he's made that way. As it is, we should be all over them before they realize what is happening. I don't think they'll give up without a fight. I'm sure Sosna won't, so shoot hard and shoot straight. We'll try to slip to the front door and crash it in. As law-abiding

189

citizens and peace officers, we must give them a chance to surrender if we get the drop on them."

"We'd be justified in blowing them from under their hats without any warning," growled Randal. "This is the first time I ever knew of anybody in this section raising a hand against a nice woman, the snake-blooded cross between a sidewinder and a skunk! But we'll do as you say, Walt, you're the boss."

They approached the Square D ranchhouse from the northwest and from the crest of the rise could see the bar of radiance streaming from the lighted front window. Slade turned a little more to the west and reached the spot where he had left Shadow the night before.

They dismounted. "They're in there, all right," said Slade in low tones. "And we've got to be in that room before they know what's happening. Otherwise we'll be in for trouble. We'll slide down to the near rear corner of the house. That way we won't have to pass the window. Right onto the porch and I'll hit the door with my shoulder. That should do it, barring slips. All set? Let's go!"

With the utmost care they crept down the slope, taking advantage of all cover against the possibility of watching eyes. Without mishap they reached the corner of the building and glided along to the front. Slade paused, peering and listening. Through an open window came a rumble of voices, but he could not hear what was said. Another moment and he was mounting the steps of the veranda, his companions crowding

190

behind him. He tensed for the final rush. And it happened!

Randal stumbled on the top step. His boots hit the floor boards with a terrific clatter. From the room sounded startled exclamations. Slade bounded forward, hit the door with his shoulder. It crashed open and he was inside the building, going sideways along the wall. He had a glimpse of men leaping to their feet. Then the room fairly exploded to the roar of sixshooters.

Over went the table and lamp. Its glass bowl shattered. Oil poured over the burning wick. Instantly a sheet of flame billowed to the ceiling, firing the curtains, licking the tinder-dry wall. Through the haze of smoke the guns bellowed. And from the rear of the house came a woman's scream, again and again.

Ducking, weaving, Slade shot with both hands at the shadowy figures looming in the murk. Behind him his companions' guns blazed. A bullet nicked the top of his shoulder and nearly hurled him off his feet with the shock. He heard Randal bark a curse, Alvarez cry out. Again that scream of terror!

Abruptly he realized there was nothing more to shoot at. Bodies were sprawled on the floor. He leaped over them, rushed through an open door and into a hall. To the right was a closed door and from behind it came a crashing sound. He hurled himself against it and it flew open and he was inside a lighted room.

Iris cowered against the wall, her eyes great pools of fright. Her dress was ripped, showing the gleam of a white shoulder. Slade bounded forward and gathered her close.

191

"You all right?" he asked.

"Yes, yes, I'm all right," she gasped. "Oh, Walt, I knew you'd come! I knew it! He tried to drag me through the window, but I fought him. When he heard your step in the hall he let me go and dived out and ran."

Slade glanced at the shattered window frame. The fugitive had taken most of the upper sash with him.

"It was Dumas?" he asked.

"Yes, it was Dumas," she replied. Before she could say more, Alvarez and Randal boiled through the door, blood streaming down the mine manager's face, the rancher limping and lurching and volleying profanity.

"Listen!" Iris exclaimed.

From outside the burning ranchhouse came the sound of fast hoofs drumming into the north.

"Take care of her," Slade called, and went through the window. Up the moonlit trail a tall horseman was riding at racing speed.

Slade sped to where he left Shadow and swung into the saddle. "Now, feller, it's up to you," he told the big black as he sent him charging to the trail. "I figure he plans to circle through Boquillas and head for the Carmen Mountains. If he makes the hills ahead of us he'll very likely give us the slip in the holes and cracks over there. Sift sand, jughead, that big bay he's forking is a good horse, but I don't think he's in your class."

Shadow proceeded to prove that he wasn't. Snorting, slugging his head above the bit, he poured his long body over the ground, his hoofs drumming, his irons striking showers of sparks from the stones. Slowly but

192

surely he closed the distance. Sosna's mile lead shrank to three-quarters, a half. When the scattered lights of Boquillas flickered into sight, the straining bay was less than a quarter of a mile ahead of the flying black.

"You're doing it, feller, you're doing it," Slade told his mount. He fingered the stock of his rifle, estimated the distance that separated him from his quarry, and shook his head. The distance was still too great for anything like accurate shooting in the deceptive moonlight and from the back of a racing horse.

"But we'll get him," he exulted. "He'll hit rough going after he turns east."

But when he reached where the trail merged with Carmen Street, Sosna did not turn east. He charged straight ahead for the swollen Rio Grande.

"What the devil!" Slade exclaimed aloud. "Does he figure to hit the river? No horse living could make it across with the water high as it is now; he's got to turn."

Nevertheless, Sosna kept right on going, his horse's irons pounding the stones. Directly ahead loomed the tower of the conveyor system, and Sosna sent his horse straight for it. In its spidery shadow he jerked his reeking, foaming mount to a halt, leaving the saddle with the animal still in motion, and whirled around. Mist was rolling in from the river and objects were blurred and indistinct, but Slade saw the gleam of metal as Sosna drew. He reached for his Winchester, slid it from the boot — long shooting for a sixgun.

Flame flickered as Sosna fired. The rifle spun from Slade's grasp, a slug imbedded in the stock. Again the

Sosna luck! A fluke hit, which wouldn't happen in a thousand times! Slade shook his tingling hand and reached for his Colt. Sosna whirled and raced to the tower. He went up the ladder like a squirrel. In sheer amazement, Slade held his fire a moment. Sosna reached the upper platform, dashed across it and vanished from the Ranger's sight.

He reappeared, a flicker of movement vaguely seen through the mist. He was dangling from the swaying, jerking cable, going hand over hand along its almost invisible length. He looked as if he were swimming in the air. Then the bulk of the tower hid him from view.

Muttering under his breath, Slade pulled Shadow to a sliding halt beside the tower. He bounded to the ladder and went up at top speed, reaching the platform. He could just make out Sosna's form dangling over the roaring river. In minutes the outlaw would reach the other side and disappear. Trying to shoot him, under the conditions, would just be a waste of precious time. Seizing the cable, Slade hurled himself in pursuit. Beneath him, the Rio Grande bellowed hungrily. About him was the swirling mist as he struggled forward, swaying between two eternities.

Sosna was making speed, but *El Halcon* was going just a little faster. The outlaw's body took on concrete form. Slade could see the forward sweep of his powerful arms, the white blur of his face as he turned his head. His own arms were already aching, his hands torn and bleeding, and he was not yet to the middle of the river.

Hand over hand, gripping the humming cable, inching forward, and slowly closing the gap! Sosna

194

glanced back again. Abruptly he swung around to face his pursuer, hooked one arm over the cable and with his free hand drew his gun.

Slade saw the pale flash, felt the wind of the passing slug. He hooked his own arm over the cable, slid his Colt from the holster and answered the outlaw's fire.

The cable jerked and swayed. The dangling forms were like two marionettes motivated by invisible strings, blasting death at each other through the misty moonlight. A bullet ripped Slade's sleeve, graining the flesh. Another tilted his hat on his head. He steadied himself an instant, took deliberate aim and squeezed the trigger. He saw Sosna's body jerk spasmodically as his arm flew up and slid from the cable. He clutched wildly with his gun hand, missed, and plummeted downward into the raging water. One arm reappeared, as if waving a sardonic farewell. Then the current gripped him and Veck Sosna, robber and killer, the man without a soul, hurtled toward where the Rio Grande thundered in its sunken gorge!

With a final glance at the tossing waters, Slade leathered his gun, struggled around and began the frightful trip back to the tower and safety. His strength was draining away, his arms were as leaden rods, without feeling, mechanically obeying the impulses from his tortured brain. The tower seemed miles away, the river close as the cable swayed and dipped. Hand over hand, a monotonous treadmill of pain, stretching onward into eternity, and with eternity close, close! His hands were still endeavoring to thrust forward when his feet struck the floor of the platform and it took him a moment to realize that he was safe. Utterly spent, he sagged against the tower uprights. Finally, his strength somewhat recovered, he floundered down the ladder and sank onto the lower platform.

A light was bobbing toward him. A moment later the night watchman appeared, holding up his lantern, peering with dilated eyes.

"*Sangre de Cristo!*" he cried. "It is *Senor* Slade! *Capitan!* Never did I see the like! Surely *El Dios* was with you this night!"

"Yes," Slade mumbled reply. "Yes, I think He was. Pedro, unlock the office and let me in. Then get a horse from the stable and ride the southwest trail till you meet Don Ramos. Tell him I am here. Wait, take my horse to the stable and get the rig off him first. Go with him, Shadow. And while you're at it, Pedro, try and pick up my Winchester over on the street just south of the tower. I don't think it's damaged much — just a slug in the stock."

"Assuredly, *Capitan*, and at once," replied the watchman.

In the office, Slade sank into a chair and with fingers that still trembled a little rolled and lighted a cigarette. He was smoking comfortably and feeling a good deal better when Alvarez and Randal burst in, the former with a handkerchief bound around his head, the rancher limping and swearing. Behind them came Iris.

"Are you all right? Did you get the blankety-blank-blank?" Randal cried.

"I don't know," Slade replied listlessly. "He went into the river. I think I drilled his arm."

"Then he's a goner," Randal declared positively. "No man could live through the canyon."

"Yes, but as I told you before, Veck Sosna isn't a man, he's a devil," Slade said. "I'll never be sure."

"Pedro told us about the finish fight on the cable," Alvarez said in awe. "He said he thought demons from *infierno* were on the loose. Guess it must have looked that way to him. I've a notion he kept well in the clear until it was all over. Couldn't blame him. Well, I guess that finishes the Faceless Riders."

"And Sosna's a goner," Randal repeated. Slade did not comment. He turned to Iris.

"How'd they trick you?" he asked.

"I hurried to the office in answer to the note supposedly written by Uncle Ramos," she replied. "I thought nothing of it; he'd called me before. Two men seized me and tied a handkerchief over my mouth and bound my hands. It happened so quickly, I didn't even have a chance to cry out. They didn't hurt me and appeared to handle me as gently as they could. They took me to the ranchhouse and placed me in a chair in that room. One man sat in another chair and watched me. When the shooting started he jumped up and ran out. Before I could try to get away, Brent Dumas rushed in. He looked like a madman. He grabbed me and tried to shove me out the window. But I fought as hard as I could to keep him from doing it. The rest you know."

"Figured to pack you off or use you for a shield," growled Randal. "Yes, the Faceless Riders are cleaned up. Those five were Square D riders. We hauled the

197

carcasses out before they roasted. They all had those blasted masks in their pockets. Well, everything ended okay. I got a hunk of meat knocked out of one leg and Al got a skinned head, nothing to worry about. Now what?"

"Now, after I've doctored my hands a little, I'm going to bed," Slade said. "I feel like I'd been dragged through a knothole and hung on a barbed wire fence to dry."

"I'll take care of your hands," Iris promised. "Let's go, Aunt Agatha will be worried to death."

Three days later the river was low enough to ford, so Slade and Randal left Boquillas.

"Offer of a good job stands indefinitely," Alvarez said.

"And I'll be waiting for you," Iris added.

"And I'll be seeing you both before long," Slade promised.

They watched him ride away, to where duty called and danger and new adventure waited.

"As the saying goes, all's well that ends well," chuckled Randal as they turned in their saddles to wave a final farewell. "The blasted Faceless Riders are done for, including that infernal Sosna."

Slade smiled and shook his head. "I wish I could be sure," he replied. "I wish I could be sure."